DAKOTA DAMNED

a novel

James Goertel

Copyright © 2019 by James Goertel
2019 L.A. Rural Trade Paperback Edition

ISBN 9781700754363

Printed in the United States of America

Book design by Chuck Muncie Cobb

For Don and Elaine from Mandan

BOOK 1

Power, Corruption, and Lies

CHAPTER ONE
Williston, North Dakota (1951)

Blindfolded and bound, Frank Lund was at least conscious again as he was being dragged across gravel by, what felt like, two sets of hands gripping and pulling at his pant legs. He was too weak from the blow to his head to put up a fight, but he mustered what little strength remained and unleashed a loud string of profanity he was sure could be heard in town. He might be going, but it wouldn't be quietly. He was Frank Lund and there would be hell to pay.

He came to rest and was now free to roll this way or that, but didn't—wouldn't think of it—and lay still instead. He held the high ground, even when he didn't. Words had always been his weapons and he drew them now.

"You may have finally grown a set of balls, Karl, but your ass has always belonged to me, and that's where I'm going to shove them when this is over."

There was no reply, only the sound of crickets and the jingle of Frank's car keys as they were pulled from his pocket.

"I own you, Karl. Always have. You don't have the guts to do what you think you're going to do."

Still there was only the crickets chirping, filling the night air, Frank thought, with a Greek chorus of clicking condemnation: *Not man enough, not man enough, not man enough...*

"As a matter of fact, why don't you just call the cops. I'm sure they could trump up a breaking and entering charge and save you the humiliation."

Then Karl spoke through the darkness.

"There won't be any cops."

Frank, not feeling the gravity of the situation, was suddenly defying it as he was hoisted from the ground at both ends of his tethered limbs.

"You know you're a dead man, Karl."

In the wake of those words, Frank felt his body swing forward, then backward, then forward once more. He was in the air the briefest of moments before his right shoulder hit hard and the darkness behind the blindfold deepened with a metallic slam.

Outside the car, Frank's muffled, but at last panicked, voice could still be heard.

"You're... a fucking... dead man, Karl."

Inside the trunk, Frank waited for a reply.

A long silence was at last broken.

"That guy died a long time ago, Frank. He's dead and gone, just a ghost in the mirror who happens to have my face."

CHAPTER TWO
Williston, North Dakota (2011)

He has always seen another man's face in the reflection of his own. But mirrors don't lie like people do, like he did when he left here. It's been twenty years since Charlie Lund walked this northwestern, once wasteland, corner of North Dakota or felt this prairie wind upon his face—this face everyone seems to know, but him.

*

"You look just like him, except for the permanent tan, of course."

Charlie Lund was here for a job and thought, *Let's get on with it already.*

The man across from him continued to shuffle through papers atop a gray, metal desk that was certainly government-issue circa early-Cold War. Charlie knew these make-shift trailer offices all too well. He'd been in dozens of them. They always smelled of lingering cigarette smoke and the stinking burn of an empty coffee pot still heating. Here in Williston, North Dakota, Cummins Energy's last concern was second-hand smoke or how fresh the coffee was. Charlie lit up and waited.

"We could use you. Haven't worked oil or gas in a while I see, but I can put you in a water truck this morning."

"What's it pay?'

"More than you were makin' in construction down in Florida this past year. I can tell you that much, Charlie. Dottie, next trailer over, will get you going on the paperwork. It starts at sixteen an hour, minimum ten hour days, ten on, two off from now 'til forever with what we're sittin' on in this basin."

Charlie stubbed out his cigarette in a small glass ashtray that sported a frosted Elks Lodge emblem at its bottom, which sat amid the paperwork and manila file folders on the desk. Wendell Krouthammer, head of personnel for Cummins Energy's Williston operation, still shuffling through the sedimentary layers of documents, breathed heavily and asked distractedly, "How's your pop?"

Charlie stood and made for the door, answering as he left.

"Don't know. Haven't seen him since I got back."

It was bright outside, so Charlie tipped the sunglasses down off his ball cap and onto the bridge of his nose. He stood there on the cobbled-together, wooden steps outside the trailer and just watched the non-stop motion of trucks and men. The snow was beginning to fall through the sunshine. It was almost Easter. He was close to turning forty-five and here he was starting all over once again. He already hated this.

CHAPTER THREE
Bismarck, North Dakota (1947)

"He's not mentally fit."

The voice came from one of the three men sitting in a back booth at the Elks Lodge in Bismarck, North Dakota. The Lund brothers leaned in across the table. The oldest, Frank, sat on one side, and on the other, the youngest, Christoph, along with middle brother Karl — who at twenty-five was five years Frank's junior and five years Christoph's senior. Christoph and Frank could have been twins— with the same round-faced, good looks and facial features, both built powerful and thick—save for the fact that Frank carried an extra thirty pounds on his frame and looked all of his thirty-years of age and even a few more. Karl, on the other hand, was tall and lean with a long face and, unlike his brothers, sported a pair of spectacles which gave him a professorial air befitting a man who had spent most of his childhood in the public library devouring literature that wasn't on the menu at home.

A waiter approached, pressed pants, white button-down shirt, open collar, apron around the waist, neat and clean. The men drew away from their close quarters into the back of the soft, overstuffed vinyl cushions on either side.

"Another round, Mr. Lund?" the waiter asked out of deference, directly and only to Frank, already knowing the answer.

"Three more drafts, Skip, and bring some jerky and beer nuts back with you."

The Missouri River cuts like a muddy, dull knife between Bismarck, the capital, and Mandan, a typically sleepy Midwest town especially circa autumn 1947. The post-war glow had faded as quickly as it had come in August of '45 across the prairie where the turn of the weather, so inextricably tied to the success or failure of crops, was more an important barometer of fortunes made and fortunes lost than the Dow Jones could ever have been. Fortunes about to be made were at the heart of the nearly-whispered conversation going on in the back booth in the Elks Lodge and had been for the past hour or so—a conversation mostly unnoticed by the members wandering in with their wives for a meal of just about anything and everything that could be broiled. Frank Lund knew them all and they all knew him. Men feared him and it was palpable in even the most casual exchanges—nervous Elks waiting on and misreading cues to either speak or shut up, whisking their wives away by the arm after stuttering excuses about an available table, a babysitter waiting at home, or a parking meter about to expire.

Frank emptied what was left of his draft and reached across the table, placed the empty glass in front of Karl, picked up Karl's half full beer and tipped it to his lips, draining it as well.

"Of course he's not mentally fit, Karl, which is why you're going to talk to him about the job."

*

"During the past winter, Congress and the late President Roosevelt
undertook a vast postwar program to harness the waters of the
entire Missouri River system with dams, levees, power houses and
irrigation canals, for the benefit of those people upstream who get
too much water and those downstream who never get enough."
Hickman Powell (1945)

*

Karl found his way out of the Elks and to his car and headed in
the direction of Frank's biddings, across the bridge back into
Mandan. As he turned off the bridge and onto Main Street, he took
note of the shadowy figures slumped in the sidewalk hollows of
closed-for-the-day storefronts, stumbling the alleys off to his left,
and shuffling in worn-off stupors outside the Corner Bar, not
ironically located on the corner at Fourth Avenue. Donald Reddeer, a
Mandan Indian, was one of the shufflers—a regular among the hung-
over ghost dancers haunting the pavement near one or another of the
town's drinking holes, looking for a handout, a bottle, or a "job."
Not the kind of jobs that found one behind a counter at a butcher
shop or loading boxcars for Burlington Northern, but the illegal kind
that white town folks wouldn't dare do themselves but still needed to
have done. Donald took full advantage of his large frame and more
accurately his massive hands which moonlighted as fists for those
willing to pay by the dollar or by the draft.

*

Snaking in and out of both immigrant and Native American
folklore of the Dakota Territory is a story which purports the
Mandan tribe's first non-native contact was with Prince Madoc, the

son of a Welsh king, some 600 years before the French Canadian trapper Sieur de la Verendrye found them encamped on the upper Missouri in the late 18th century. The prince, myth recounts, sailed west to escape the wars his father was waging and eventually returned from the New World, only to leave again with one hundred souls in tow to establish colonies, but this time never to return nor be heard from again. The Mandan's language and appearance were far different from neighboring tribes, the Hidatsa and the Arikara. But it was their earthen lodges that really set them apart and seemed to mimic Welsh constructions of Prince Madoc's 12th century. Considering all the heartache of the smallpox epidemics of 1837-38 the tribe endured coupled with their inability to curb the advances of the white man over the subsequent decades, it seems only fitting that Sieur de la Verendrye found them in their historic tribal lands on the upper Missouri along the banks of two of its tributaries: the Heart and the Knife Rivers.

*

Legend, truth, or an unclear mix of both, this oft romanticized, ultimately brutal conjoined history of the Mandan and the white man was far from Karl's mind as he parked and stepped out into the long light of another all-too-short North Dakota autumn, looking to ease the pain of pure longing and the hollowness of separation scarring his own heart. Multiple trips to the Williston area, two hundred and twenty-five miles to the west, had taken him away from an all-consuming but forbidden love here in Mandan— forbidden as far as Frank was concerned, all consuming as far as Karl's heart had reminded him again and again as he drove over and over, back and forth, the lonely stretch between Mandan and Williston, trips the past four months to the Williston Basin where he had been sent by Frank to look into leasing and buying land under which some geologists, the large independent oil company Amerada, and a few hopeful entrepreneurs speculated there might be oil and quite a bit of it.

Karl had collected a handful of lesser leases at Frank's behest in the previous months, but not the critical one his older brother prized for a tract of land owned and farmed by a middle-aged widower, Harlan Andersson. Harlan, the only son among six children of a turn-of-the-century, immigrant homesteading family from Smaland, Sweden, worked the significant acreage just outside Williston, where he also lived with the nineteen-year-old daughter he had raised by himself over the past two decades' boom and bust years' wheat production. The widower hadn't liked Karl one bit and had flat out declined to even consider the Lund offer not once, but twice, refusing to sell or even lease his land, sending Karl away the second time with the sweep of a shotgun while calling him a carpetbagger from Bismarck which was correct on only one account. Karl was from Mandan, not Bismarck.

Karl pulled his flapping sport coat close in across his chest with one hand in a futile gesture against the prairie wind whipping a cold front into Mandan and seemingly right down Main Street as he headed for the bar.

CHAPTER FOUR

Williston, North Dakota (2011)

The truth was Charlie had already tried to see his father even though he'd been back in Williston less than twenty-four hours. He had seen his father, in fact, but his father had not seen him. After getting into town, he'd driven out to the failing, falling down farmhouse there on Highway 1804, not too far down from the 4 Mile Bar, where he'd first stopped to down some courage, but had left with something less. The light had been on in the kitchen and he had seen his father's frail figure shuffling back and forth. Charlie had idled on the highway for a few minutes, staring at the house where he had been raised before losing his nerve and heading back to the bar.

His father had never been able to convince his mother to move and now she was dead, near eighteen years gone, years Charlie had spent in California, Oregon, Texas, and Maine, before settling in Florida. She was buried in Williston, in a grave next to her own father's —a grave that in fact did not hold the actual body of Charlie's grandfather, a man he had never met. Charlie had always thought maybe, just maybe, that's what had killed her long before the cancer added its cruel footnote.

But now Charlie didn't want to think about any of them for the time being or about the real reason he had returned from his self-imposed exile. He just wanted to drive the water truck back and forth between the filling station and whatever frack site they radioed him to take his load. He liked feeling numb; a feeling he could get real easy in a truck with just a foot against the gas pedal, eyes focused only on the windshield in front of him. *No more mirrors*, he thought to himself as he headed back into the main site.

There were some familiar faces at the site, guys who had never left Williston, who he had gone to school with, drunk with, fought with. But there were more unfamiliar faces, mean faces with dirty looks and crooked lips even the muck and oil of long days in the field couldn't hide. They were from all over the country, hell-bent to make it, even if it meant displacing themselves and their families. But most were here alone—sending a check back to a pregnant girlfriend or a wife holding down the fort somewhere with three or four kids running around her all day. Charlie could sense it all—their desperation, their last ditch efforts for a better life, and their lack of consideration or respect for the locals. He could intuit it from the way they dragged on their generic brand cigarettes, the way they stood at the trough in the communal, twenty-men-at-a-time Porta-Johnny trailer holding onto the one thing they thought defined them as men, and from their foul-mouthed comments for any female employee doing administrative paperwork who was brave or stupid enough to leave the safety of a company trailer for any reason. But Charlie admitted to himself that, in a way, he was one of them. He was here to make a buck at any cost. The difference being he had no one back in Florida he had to send half his paycheck to and that he had no problem keeping his ogling to a minimum for he ogled not at all. Charlie knew he was smarter than most of the guys working the site. He was sure none of these Neanderthals had read Nietzsche, Baudelaire, or Faulkner. But, he also recognized they were smarter than him in some respects. They knew who they were and their sense of morality, ethics, and fair play began and ended with their balls, not their brains. Charlie couldn't help but wonder how sweet that must be, to truly not give a shit. He had spent his entire adult life trying to live up to the expectations of a father, an education, and a face that wasn't entirely his own.

*

The fumes were much worse than usual. Shannon Dilfer went around the inside of her trailer opening windows until she made her way to the front door, the only door for that matter, pulling it open and then propping its screen door wide before stepping onto the stoop and into the cold air holding snow flurries carried this way and that with the prairie wind.

She held an unlit cigarette between the middle and pointer fingers of her left hand and in a moment of hesitation thought better of lighting it right there outside the trailer. She walked up the rutted dirt drive and headed for the shelter of a dilapidated tool shed held together by mostly rust, but still standing in spite of two decades' worth of Dakota wind, freeze, thaw, and rain. She slid open one side of the shed's double slider, stepped in, lit the cigarette, and took a long, hard drag as she surveyed the one hundred and eighty degrees of landscape afforded her from this perspective. She could see parts of at least three of the four large farms that surrounded her pauper's five acre plot. This postage stamp of land in the vast expanse of the prairie acted as a none-too-gentle reminder of the failures of both her genealogy and her education. It was true, a lot of dumb-asses she'd gone to school with had gotten plenty rich from leasing or outright selling their land to the likes of Cummins Energy and other outfits— folks with as little acreage as her own. The fact though was she didn't own the land the trailer sat on and so, could not legally lease it. Considering her little place was surrounded by leased land, she figured Cummins would just suck out whatever was under her while they were at it. She took a last drag just as the wind shifted and filled the shed with the smell of methane. There was never a lack of tears for Shannon, fumes or no fumes. She gagged a moment and then dry-heaved into her throat causing her eyes to water.

CHAPTER FIVE

Fort Berthold Reservation, North Dakota (1947)

Frank did not rise from his seat as others mostly did when wishing to be recognized at the council meeting on the Fort Berthold Reservation. The reservation towns of Van Hook and Sanish were soon going to be underwater as a result of the Garrison Dam project. Frank and his company, Lund Cement, had a vested interest in the project, standing to make more than a pretty penny with pending contracts as a primary supplier of concrete. He had attended previous meetings, listened to the bickering, taking note of who was for, who was against the dam. Information was power and Frank wasn't about to let one little, two little, three little Indian tribes get in the way of his potential payday. Frank could also see the writing on the dam wall even though the first yard of concrete had yet to be poured. New towns, such as the one being proposed here at the council meeting, would be springing up on the edges of the project and he was hell bent to grab as many contracts for Lund Cement as he could get his hands on—whatever that might take.

The reservation's Three Affiliated Tribes, as they were known, including the Mandan, Hidatsa, and Arikara Nation, were to be compensated by the U.S. Government for the 150,000 acres of reservation land affected by the project. But the $5.1 million earmarked for the Three Affiliated Tribes was far short of the $22 million they had wanted. For some on the reservation, the dam project was less about the money and more about another broken treaty with Washington, D.C. All of this was at play this evening, and things had been pretty heated for the past hour, with tribal elders trading barbs with one another, government officials, and the small amount of press present, when Frank finally spoke up.

"Why don't you just combine the names Van Hook and Sanish and call the new town Vanish?"

There was a ripple of laughter from the portion of the room consisting of white men in starched shirts and neckties. A few of the council members got up and walked out. The eyes of those still present all turned to Frank as he rose, placed his fedora on his head, canting it just so, which had an ambiguous visual effect that was simultaneously mobster and G-Man.

"Let's hope a matter as trifling as a name doesn't hold up the obvious extension of the tenets of Manifest Destiny. Good day, gentlemen."

Frank made his way through the room toward the exit, but paused a moment before pushing on out through the door, adding, "And everyone else."

He could hear the rumbling and the grumbling in response to his comments as he paused just outside the corrugated tin structure to light a cigar, before getting into the back of a waiting, brand new, customized Delahaye 135 convertible.

Frank was halfway back to Bismarck before the council decided to take at least part of his recommendation voting in favor of New Town as the name for the new administrative center for the reservation. Frank loosened his tie and poured himself a bourbon from the custom Cadillac's bar setup. He rolled the amber liquid back and forth across the ice cubes and smiled, feeling quite pleased with himself.

"I wonder if Karl is having any luck with that human totem pole. What do you think, Christoph?"

Christoph eyed Frank in the rearview mirror as he drove with one hand and smoked with the other.

"Pour me one of those, would ya?"

Frank downed his drink in one long tip of the glass. "Just drive, baby brother. Just drive," rolling off Frank's tongue like a half-hearted 'mush' without the usual crack of the whip upon the sled dog's flesh.

CHAPTER SIX
Williston, North Dakota (2011)

"How about a beer?"

The voice was familiar, too familiar, and Charlie turned as he landed on terra firma after eight hours behind the wheel of the water truck. He hadn't seen Dawes in almost twenty years, but Dawes hadn't changed all that much and looked much as he had back in the day when they had run themselves ragged chasing the available and sometimes not available women of Williston. Dawes had a cowboy gait from a youth spent on horseback rounding up cattle on his father's ranch and he was as wiry and chiseled now as he had been back then.

"I didn't think I needed a drink until your ugly mug showed up. Where are you watering these days, Dawes?"

"Anywhere I ain't been banned from yet."

"That must be most of Williston then. What's the plan?"

"We can start with the bottle in my truck."

"High class as usual. You haven't changed a bit."

"You tried, but apparently it didn't work out if you're back in this suck-ass excuse for a town."

"I suppose we don't get paid for shooting the shit, so let me punch out."

"With that college degree of yours I figured they'd of made you a foreman, but I guess this is how it goes when you get a B.S. in B.S."

"Fuck you, Dawes."

"Fuck you, Charlie. Good to see you again."

"Good to be seen, I guess, by certain people."

"She's still around you know."

"No, I didn't and wasn't asking."

"Fair enough, friend," Dawes managed from his mouth after moving the tobacco plug in his cheek from one side to the other.

CHAPTER SEVEN
North Dakota

The big sky dwarfs the land with its wide tides of rolling wheat.
The sun plays with light differently in the prairie expanse. The
summers are a gift given begrudgingly by the bleak and brutal
Dakota winters with their snow in September, snow in late April,
and floods waiting in the spring thaw eager to jump banks along the
Missouri, along its length and tributaries: Tobacco Garden Creek,
James River, Cow Creek, Crooked River, Bad River, Arrow Creek,
and the Heart and Knife Rivers. The land holds nothing, holds
everything. Scandinavian immigrants of the late 19th century, with
no time for déjà vu, must have seen something familiar, felt
something au courant about the homesteads of the Dakota Territory.
The Norwegians, Germans, and Swedes who flocked to the area in
the Dakota Boom of 1870 through 1880 ground out a hardscrabble
existence, one inexorably tied to the weather and a wealth the land
never fully relinquished. The gold mining boom, more like a bust, of
the 1870's in the Black Hills of what would become South Dakota,
did in fact serve to fuel the populating of the area. But above all else,
low cost land via the Homestead Act of 1862, eventually planted
from one end to the other with the area's cash crop, wheat, was the

draw. The one hundred and sixty acres provided by the act could be just enough or far too little to provide the milk and honey existence promised in government ads offering cheap land, a new start, and a future rife with the spoils of democracy. The land of the Dakota Territory, which officially became two states in November of 1889, was more like a feudal lord, especially in the drought years of the 1880's when wheat prices tumbled, carrying with them, in their cascade, dreams more like mirages, shattering them upon the soil turned to stone cracking beneath immigrant feet. But salvation arrived in the form of a golden spike, driven into the ground in early September of 1883 by former President Ulysses S. Grant at Gold Creek in central Montana, thus completing the main line of the Northern Pacific Railroad running from the Great Lakes to the Pacific Ocean and directly through and across North Dakota.

CHAPTER EIGHT
Mandan, North Dakota (1947)

Inside the dark bar, smoke from cigarettes and cigars hung in the singular shaft of light from the dirty window at the near end of the tap room. Butch Geissler, the owner, pulled drafts for the railroad workers now done with their seven to three-thirty shifts at the Northern Pacific railyard directly across from the Corner Bar and sprawling along Main Street in Mandan. Karl took a stool and gestured for Donald Reddeer to take one as well.

"You can't bring him in here, Karl. I won't serve him," Geissler huffed.

"Oh yeah, Butch? Maybe we oughta call Frank and see what he says."

"Jesus, why do you have to be such a hard ass?"

"Because we own the building, remember Butch?"

"I serve one of 'em and the next thing you know they'll all be in here, stumblin' around, makin' passes at the women. I don't need that kind of trouble, it's bad for business. Please."

Karl, calm and cool, but secretly on edge whenever he had to do Frank's dirty work, acknowledged the comment with a reassuring nod and a smile. Then turned the tables.

"You can either pour the beers or give me change for the pay phone."

Butch avoided conflict with Frank at all costs and with a huff pulled two mugs from beneath the bar with one hand and hit the tap with the other, letting golden liquid flow into one and then the other.

Donald smiled, having enjoyed seeing Butch put in his place, and chimed in, "And fill'em both to the top, Geissler."

The room buzzed a bit with snickering and sudden hushed conversation as Geissler begrudgingly began pulling the drafts. A baseball game, the final and deciding game of the World Series between the New York Yankees and the Brooklyn Dodgers, chattered in the background from an unseen radio. Matty, a tall Swede and a tough guy from the railyard, pushed away from the bar, stood, and turned toward Donald, hovering above and behind him.

"I ain't drinking with no scalp collector."

Donald looked directly at Karl, smiled, and in one swift motion pushed the stool out from under himself and into Matty, who fell forward just in time to meet Donald's heavy right fist as it arced upward from below into Matty's chin. There was a cracking sound audible above the game, above the surprised gasp of patrons at both the tables and along the bar. Matty fell back on the worn, aged timbers of the floor and groaned slightly, eyes closed. Railyard workers rose almost simultaneously from a table near the altercation and leaned their sobering body language toward Donald, coiled to pounce in tandem, until Karl relieved them of the notion by pulling a Smith & Wesson M&P .38 Special from a shoulder holster secreted beneath his sport coat and pointing it, steady and fully extended, at them.

"Sit down, boys. How about a round for the bar?" offered Karl, dropping the dramatic in favor of the diplomatic.

Karl holstered the handgun, adding, "Beer and a shot for everybody, Butch, and put it on Frank's tab... but I wouldn't."

There was a ripple of relieved laughter as everyone settled back into their pursuit of a late afternoon drunk. Matty pulled himself up to the bar, moved down a few stools and leaned past Donald's profile. He squared his now un-square jaw to Karl while slipping a cigarette from a pack onto his lower, bloodied lip and lisped, "You're a rotten son of bitch, Karl. Nothin' but Frank's trained monkey."

Karl felt the sting of his comment more deeply than anyone could ever know, but knew the Mattys of the world were easily put in their place.

"Maybe so, Matty, but you ought to be more worried about having that lip fixed before the queers in Bismarck get a load of that lisp."

A burst of laughter was soon replaced by the rhythmic, lulling cadence of the baseball broadcast. The barroom at last faded to its own dark corners, leaving Karl to shed a light for Donald as to why the free libation had been offered in the first place. As with the baseball game filling the air around them, there was always a catch.

CHAPTER NINE

Williston, North Dakota (2011)

Dawes maneuvered what was left of his 1990 F-150 in between, around, and down through a man-camp of RVs a few miles from the main drilling site. With no work to be had in the post-mortgage-bubble-burst of the previous few years, Williston was a bright spot in an economy still limping along on promises and predictions. The stories out of these drilling encampments, the same type that had popped up all over the Marcellus Shale region back East, all told a similar tale of desperation and sudden, possibly lingering, destitution not only for working folks, but educated ones as well. Now, some of them, from both sides of the economic tracks, were here—living the Miller High Life in good natured circles of folding chairs setup outside their RVs, campers, and conversion vans. The devil had nearly caught them all as they had waited in the limbo of their unemployment purgatories, but the "drill-baby-drill" ethos of energy producers had saved them. The oil companies, America's ready-made villains, had been supplanted by the stockbrokers, bankers, and mortgage lenders of Wall Street and the government's $700 billion dollar and counting bailout. It was one thing to help keep American icons like General Motors and Chrysler in the black, but a whole other notion to sew the hard earned tax dollars of the working class into the already golden bathing suits of corporate America's Ivy League snobs and their inner circles of well-to-do and well-connected cronies. The oil companies on the other hand didn't need a bailout. In fact, there was more than enough readily available capital to begin going after the hardest to reach energy resources that places like the Marcellus Shale and the Bakken Formation had to offer.

The informal 'town' here on the outskirts of Williston reminded Charlie of Depression-era photos of the Bonus Army encampments in Washington, D.C. in the early 1930's, except which, upon closer inspection, revealed a well-fed, well-watered, and convivial army of oil field hands and handlers. And with a Wal-Mart just down the road, this army looked almost downright well-dressed in their brand new Wrangler Jeans, Timberland work boots, and Carhartt jackets.

"Place looks clean," slipped from Charlie lips.

"Just dirty enough to keep it interesting," Dawes chimed in as he put the truck in park, cut the engine, and pulled a bottle from beneath the seat, passing it to Charlie with the invitation, "Here, suck on this awhile and it'll start to look like the fuckin' suburbs."

Charlie took the non-descript bottle half filled with an equally non-descript clear liquid, uncapped it and tipped it to his lips, taking a mouthful. He struggled to swallow but did and tilted his head toward the chewed-up cab ceiling, closing his eyes, unable to suppress a full facial wince.

"Jesus god damn Christ, what is this shit? Did you make it in one of your work boots?"

"That's grain, old buddy. We always drank this shit back in the day."

"That was twenty years ago, Dawes. This shit will put me to sleep now if it doesn't burn a hole in my liver first. Christ almighty."

Dawes began to laugh, laugh hard, and through it offered, "I got shit to keep you awake too, amigo." Then, from an inside jacket pocket, he produced a sandwich baggie and handed it to Charlie.

"What's this?" Charlie asked, lifting the baggie toward the windshield and its low glow of reflected shine from work lights running off generators set up around the various social circles.

"That's methamphetamine, brother. Keep your ass awake all the way through a ten day shift and then some."

"This isn't the Williston I remember."

"Like I said, just dirty enough to keep it interesting. Get you laid with a phone call too. Just like that," Dawes bragged, adding a snap of his fingers for effect.

Charlie handed the baggie back with a, "I'm good," and then capped the bottle and put it between him and Dawes.

"No problem, but eventually you'll be wonderin' where I get my stuff. But no worries, I can get you hooked up when the time comes. Hey, I got a twelve pack behind your seat. Let's grab it and see what my Okie friends are gettin' into. A lot of boys are up here from Oklahoma, the o-riginal boom and bust."

Dawes chattered on as they got out of the truck. Now Charlie understood why Dawes had been talking non-stop for the past hour. He was cranking on meth and Charlie knew enough from the cocaine scene down in South Florida to recognize it was the dope talking, figuratively and in a way, literally. Charlie grabbed the twelve-pack from behind the seat and followed on after Dawes, walking by several different groups of drivers, drillers, haulers, and pipe fitters, before landing in front of a big Winnebago where a dozen men were sitting around drinking and bullshitting. They recognized Dawes and one of them, an obese hick in a few layers of brand new flannel shirts beneath coveralls, sporting a flat top and wire rim glasses to small for his face, spoke up.

"Hey, Dawes. Who's the injun?"

Dawes chuckled a nervous chuckle and answered, "Old buddy of mine. Charlie. He grew up around here."

The fat hick turned his attention to Charlie.

"Sorry to hear that, Tonto. You got ugly women around here and the nightlife ain't nothin' to write home about. That's for sure."

Charlie stood dead still, sinking into the sudden silence of the gathering.

"Well," the fat hick coughed up, breaking the impasse, "you gonna pass around some of those beers or do a war dance?"

The laughter from the group bounced back and forth off the hard sides of the RVs and campers for what seemed an implausible amount of time and Charlie could still hear it in his head when he bedded down for the night at the motel down the road, taking Dawes up on an offer to share the room and the cost until he found his own place.

*

Shannon woke up early, awakened as usual by the passing din of perpetual truck traffic. The constant and pervasive rumbling of the water trucks for the frack sites never really stopped for any appreciable amount of time. It was a 24-7 operation. Six months prior there had been a super cell threatening to drop an unusual-for-this-neck-of-the-woods twister on Williston and the surrounding area, which had precipitated the only noticeable cessation of activity along the road outside her trailer. Otherwise the sound of birds tweeting, singing at her feeders had long since been replaced by the diesel-fueled roll of thunder along what had always been an otherwise deserted stretch of road outside of Williston.

She worked a filter into the coffee pot, filled it with what was left from the can of Folgers, and dumped twice the required amount of water into the maker in what had become a ritual to stretch every conceivable resource she had. She hadn't worked since being fired from the Lunch Box in Williston three months before and the unemployment check was always nearly gone by the time the fifteenth of each month arrived. She had looked for work, waitressing work at other eateries in town, but her reputation preceded her it seemed; a reputation for drinking too much at night, showing up late or not at all for work, and for her bad attitude when she did. Twenty years of threadbare employment in the food service industry had come to a crashing end the day she plucked a smoldering cigarette out of an ashtray from one of the tables she was working and stuck it into the pancake stack of an oilfield worker who had remarked that he enjoyed the view of her 'sweet ass' as she hustled back and forth to keep coffee cups filled and plates cleared. She had been hit on plenty of times over the years while slinging hash for tips, but the Williston boom had brought in a crowd she could not stomach. She was no activist, didn't really understand all of the issues of fracking that some in town were so up in arms over, but she longed for the simpler, more subtle Williston that seemed to have disappeared with the appearance of Cummins Energy and other oil companies in her little prairie town. She knew she had a great ass and so did a good portion of the born and bred in Williston males, but local lechery had been replaced by an invading army of criminals, deadbeats, and deviants hell-bent on bedding every woman walking upright atop the Bakken Formation. Local teenage pregnancy rates had doubled since Cummins Energy had come courting. These overpaid and under-mannered barbarians with their dicks without conscience were her complaint, not the now flammable tap water percolating into coffee here in her sad, little kitchen.

The TV blared in the background with the sound of a weather forecast. She had taken to turning it up to a deafening volume to drown out the sound of the water trucks' back and forth procession outside her door, but it did not keep her from hearing the sound of a vehicle pulling up the driveway. She peered through one of the missing slats of the plastic blind barely holding on above the window near the door. A Cummins Energy pick-up sat outside, white exhaust billowing from its tailpipe into the spring season's predictably cold, but frigid by Lower Forty-Eight standards, April air. Nobody in their right mind ever shut off a vehicle during a Williston winter which, more often than not, lasted well past Easter. Two men, each encased in a parka, got out of the truck, paused a moment to look over the property, then made their way to the front stoop. Shannon pulled back from the blind and took a deep breath.

CHAPTER TEN
Mandan, North Dakota (1947)

*

But what of the future? Will the day come when we will need all the cheap power we can produce? Those confident of North Dakota's future say "yes." Pessimists say "no."
- Anonymous (editorial from The Bismarck Tribune, 1945)

*

"How will I get there?"

The Corner Bar was now full. The railyard workers from the seven to three-thirty shift were well into their third hour. Karl and Donald had moved to a table in a curtained-off back room. Donald was still working the free draught beer courtesy of Karl. Plates of dinner had long since been emptied, but still littered the table top. Donald's question had come out as a slur. Karl had him where he wanted him, half in the bag. Donald would be desperate to keep his drunk going, hoping he'd be leaving with a coveted bottle in a brown paper bag.

"You'll have a car."

"How much?"

"A hundred."

"Fifty now, fifty after," Donald huffed, straightening himself in an effort to assert an authority that didn't exist.

"A bottle in a bag now for your time listening to a conversation that didn't take place. A hundred and a case of beer when it's done. Understand?"

Donald nodded, more than willing to compromise now that a bottle had been promised for the cold night to come.

"A hundred and a case, hmmm. I'll have to think about it. How about that bottle then?"

"The bottle is for an answer now."

"Then the answer is yes."

Karl extended his hand, but it was not met by one from Donald.

"Shaking hands is what cost us our tribal lands then and what will bury our reservations beneath the Missouri now."

"I can't argue with that," Karl agreed.

On the way out of the bar Karl stopped and motioned to Geissler who was busy pouring drafts. He pointed to a bottle of whiskey, ordering, "Put one of those in a bag."

"Is it for Reddeer?"

"You didn't hear it from me, Butch, but Frank's wife has been eyeing this building for that flower shop she wants to open."

Geissler grumbled as he grabbed the bottle off the shelf and slipped it into a brown paper bag.

"I wonder what your old man would have said if he'd lived to see how his boys turned out," Geissler stabbed back at Karl as he handed him the bottle, only releasing it once he had finished saying his peace.

"The dead don't speak. Something you ought to keep in mind before you open your mouth again," Karl shot back in rebut while handing the bottle to Donald, adding, "You know, you could get in a lot of trouble for serving Indians, Dutch."

Geissler fumed as Karl and Donald exited into the failing autumn light, leaving behind the dimly lit bar and a conversation best left behind in its shadows.

Karl soon found himself behind the wheel of his car and driving past John Paul Hoff's house on 10th Avenue. He drove up and down the street again and again—each time trying to peer into the house through evening windows lit with the yellow of incandescent light from lamps switched on in different rooms now that dusk was finally finding its way to the horizon. He parked across the street—not directly but between the Hoff home and the neighbor's. He turned the car off and sat awhile watching a cloud of red-winged blackbirds swirl, dive, and rise in an unfathomably tight formation here and there in the sky before disappearing to roost until another morning came calling for their daylight rhythms to wake. Lost in their dance, Karl did not notice the man who was now standing next to his driver-side window. The man's rapping knuckles against the glass broke his reverie.

Karl jolted in his seat and he squinted into the indecipherable face of a man who was heavily backlit by the streetlight. The window muffled the man's voice, but it did not matter, the accent was immediately familiar to Karl with its thick German tongue offering a version of English.

"I said I'll have you arrested for loitering."

It was John Paul Hoff—a prominent City Councilman and a shoe-in for the open State Senate seat for which he had been campaigning the past year. He was a pillar of the community. His resume included stints as the police commissioner in Bismarck and the mayor of Mandan. He had only withdrawn from a run for governor, which he would have won handily, when his son was badly wounded in combat at the Battle of the Bulge and lingered in an English hospital for three months before succumbing to his injuries. Hoff had been a yardmaster, a semi-pro boxer, and an immigrant from Hitler's Germany after the Brown Shirts had turned up the heat on Germans sympathetic to their Jewish friends and neighbors. In fewer than twenty years, he'd remade himself as a politician, becoming an American citizen and embracing with a bear hug befitting his size the original and pure tenets of the American democratic system. In short, he was not a man to be trifled with.

He represented two stumbling blocks to the Lund brothers: one economic, the other personal. John Paul Hoff opposed the Garrison Dam project and had personally been able to stall its progress for a time through his network of powerful connections. But more importantly, he opposed the relationship between his twenty-one year old daughter, Marilyn, and Karl. Despite Hoff's best efforts, it looked as though the dam was about to become inevitable, an unstoppable reality, and a personal and political defeat for him. There had been a ceremonial groundbreaking just two days ago to officially kick off the project. The ice jams on the Missouri in the spring and the flooding of three million acres along the river which followed had resulted in damages in excess of $100 million and the loss of twenty-six lives, guaranteeing the Garrison would be built. The Lund brothers would get what they wanted on this account, but John Paul was determined that Karl Lund would not become his son-in-law. A thought which repelled him more than a dam built upon another broken treaty.

John Paul pulled at the door handle, but the car door was locked. He leaned down close, nearly pressing his face against the window. Karl just stared at him, Hoff's voice becoming nothing more than a frequency—like that of a refrigerator hum in a room that goes unnoticed, white noise behind the fever dream of living. Karl noticed how much Hoff looked like an immigrant. With the right hat, he could have been a conductor on a train rumbling through the breathtaking topography of the Bavarian region of Germany. He was handsome with a full head of perfectly coiffed, salt and pepper hair, cherubic cheeks, and a strong, masculine if uneventful nose, save for it being just slightly askew at the bridge from having been broken in the boxing ring. Karl was sure, though, that Hoff had broken his share. Marilyn had more angular features; there was an innate sadness to her face, and her doe eyes, big, brown and somehow tragic, made it hard not to want to hold her, to save her from something; though he wasn't sure what that 'something' was.

In the midst of John Paul's tirade, Marilyn appeared over his shoulder at a distance, standing on the doorstep, and lit by a porch light that added an ethereal glow. Her blonde hair, a halo on fire, framed her pale face which seemed in stark contrast to the deep red of the lipstick kissed upon her lips. Although he could not hear John Paul anymore, he heard Marilyn with a clarity that seemed to defy the distance and the car window between them.

"Daddy, don't. Stop. Please."

And then he was driving, her voice reverberating in his brain for miles, her face a home movie across his windshield. When he finally stopped well outside of Mandan, near a stretch of the Missouri, on a small plot of land with a cabin his father had built a decade before the Great Depression, he got out and stared at the black water for a long time thinking it would not be John Paul who would keep him from realizing his love for Marilyn. It would be Frank, for it had always been Frank who had stood between him and every happiness his life had let him glimpse so far.

CHAPTER ELEVEN
Williston, North Dakota (2011)

*

"My people have always been friendly with the whites and never carried open warfare to them. The right side of my heart is still friendly and happy toward them. I sit here now and see no danger in front of me. Neither is there death standing behind me."
- Little Owl, full blooded Mandan
(From an address to the American Indian Federation, Mandan, 1939)

*

"Get up, man."

Charlie could feel himself being shaken awake. The room was cold, despite the fact the motel room heater had been on all night cycling on, then off, over and over with a degree change here, a degree change there. He'd left Florida for this. He'd even become accustomed to the insufferable summers. In fact he liked the feeling of a full sweat brought on by ninety-five percent humidity hanging in ninety-five degree air. For all the years he had been away though, in the different locales around the country, he had never once felt at home. Back in the frosty grip of North Dakota, he already felt a sense of place that had been missing. The memories weren't good here, but they were still here, had been waiting all along to reconnect with their biology, their chemistry. They had that lived-in feeling, the soft and the scratch of a lifetime ago—cotton and wool all at once. And even if it were still too early to embrace them fully, he knew they were there for him and it gave Charlie a sense of hope. A feeling he had not had in a very long time.

"They fired some black guy last week for being late. Didn't fire him 'cause he was black, but because he was late. Didn't like the motherfucker at all. It's one thing to have spics and good old boys fuckin' our women, but that—heh—not that shit man."

Fucking Dawes. Charlie was already regretting that he'd been friendly to him again right off the bat.

"You better snort some of this shit, coffee ain't gonna cut it for the next ten hours."

Charlie opened his eyes to a baggie full of white powder being waved in front of his face.

"Get up, bitch. I'm gonna start the truck. Motel's got some donuts and shit they set out every morning in the office. It ain't good, but it's free. Meet you down there, boss."

The door closing behind Dawes with a slam was an exclamation point upon an ongoing verbal onslaught that was unused to punctuation. Charlie sat up, stood up and having slept in his clothes, simply slipped on his work boots, leaving them unlaced, making his way to the door, opening it and stepping into a white-out of sunlight in stark contrast to the blackout of the heavily curtained Room 119. He hoped there was coffee to go along with the half-assed complimentary breakfast. He had no intention of starting his day out of a Ziploc baggie.

*

The coffee Charlie had procured back at the motel office actually looked more like weak tea water and wasn't hot enough in its Styrofoam cup to warm his ungloved hand, but Charlie gulped it down anyway as Dawes chattered on, occasionally stopping to stick a licked thumb into the baggie of meth and then under his flared right nostril. The sunlight had already given way to a sudden squall, gray replacing the early morning blue that had waited outside the motel room about a half hour before. Dawes pulled the truck into a makeshift parking lot for the employees of Cummins Energy, put the truck in park, and, like most things that he pulled from the inside of his jacket pocket, produced yet another quizzical item.

"Here. Piss in this."

Dawes handed him an old, empty prescription pill bottle.

"What?"

"Piss in it. You just downed that whole big jigger of coffee, you must have to piss, dude."

"You're a fucking lunatic. I'm not pissing in some old drug bottle of yours."

"Come on, man, I got a bad feeling my number's up. They've been pullin' guys out of trucks for the past week, handin' them a container, and sendin' them to a Porta-Johhny to piss into it."

"It's called random drug testing, which you would fail by the way."

"No shit. But you wouldn't, which is why I need your piss. Come on, I need this job."

Charlie grabbed the tiny bottle with a huff. "You fucking owe me. I haven't been back two days and I'm already bailing your sorry ass out. It's just like twenty years ago."

"Good times."

"No, not good times," Charlie mustered as he worked the tip of his penis just above the rim of the pill bottle, making sure not to let it come in contact with who-knew-what?

An awkward fifteen seconds passed, but Charlie was grateful for the silence. Finally, Dawes had shut up.

"Here," Charlie offered with a thrust of his hand, a little of his piss cresting and splashing on Dawes' blue jeans.

"Jesus, fucking, Christ—careful. That's a six month pass to easy livin', my brother."

"You don't look it, but you must be retarded. There's something not right with you."

"Not what the ladies say. I couldn't get my dong into that tiny ass pill bottle like you did, chief."

Dawes laughed until he began to choke, then cough, hacking up phlegm so badly he had to roll down his window to spit.

And there she was, Shannon. God knows how long she'd been outside the steamed over window, but there she was now and twenty years collapsed like a dead star into a black hole just like that for Charlie.

"I just knew I'd find you two together." I didn't believe it when they told me you were back in town. Get out of the truck you rotten son of a bitch. They're taking my land."

"You mean my father's land."

"You're not even back in town two days and you already got the old man to break the agreement we've had since you skipped out of here. Get out of that truck, now!"

"Haven't seen him."

"Liar."

From her side Shannon produced a baseball bat and before any words could stutter their way out of the well-methed Dawes, she had clubbed off the side mirror.

"Jesus Christ, Shannon. What the fuck are you doing? Hit him, not my god damned truck, you bitch."

"Go ahead Dawes, say 'bitch' again."

"Bitch."

Shannon reared back with the bat, but before she could swing, Dawes rocketed the door open and into her, leaving her in a groaning pile in the gravel covered parking area.

"Dawes, damn you, man," and with that Charlie was out of the truck.

By the time Charlie reached the other side of the truck, Shannon was back on her feet and swinging. The bat connected with a crack, meeting Charlie's left knee cap. Before he could react he was down on the ground, pain shooting up and down his left leg. Shannon raised the bat over her head, but her momentum was interrupted by

Dawes who put his shoulder into her rib cage, sending them both to the ground.

Dawes was the first to speak as they all lay there, splayed in the parking lot as a group of fitters, riggers, and drivers began to gather around the wounded. "You fuckin' made me drop my piss, you bitch," his screaming words carrying on the crystalline air far enough to draw the attention of some management types. He wouldn't have to worry about a random drug test today. An hour later, in Wendell's trailer, he was sent home for the day. Charlie was given two weeks off without pay, but refused to press charges against Shannon, who just glared at him until the police finished their report and escorted the three of them off-site.

Charlie stood, leaning against Dawes truck to keep weight off his left leg as Shannon made her way to her rusted out, 1976 Gran Torino, a car that was already ten years old when Charlie had bought it for her in better times.

"That thing still runnin'?"

Shannon turned on a dime and spat back, "Yeah, just like the guy who bought it for me."

"Let me buy you breakfast."

"I'd rather eat my own shit. Go to hell, Charlie."

Shannon opened the driver-side door which creaked badly, got in, started the Torino, and pulled out with a powerful crush of the accelerator, throwing gravel in a volatile spray that pelted Charlie and Dawes' truck.

"That bitch is still crazy, Charlie," Dawes noted with a whistle for emphasis that fell flat amidst the rumbling and gear grinding of trucks coming and going from the site.

"Shut up, Dawes. Just shut up already."

"I saved your ass. She was gonna beat you to death. You oughta buy me a beer. Got the day off you know. Come on."

"I'm walkin'."

"It's three miles back to your truck."

Charlie ignored Dawes and hobbled off. A little way down the road it hit him that Dawes had called him an asshole as he walked away. Dawes was right. He was an asshole. He'd left in the middle of the night twenty years before, leaving Shannon to fend for herself. There were a lot of hard years on her face. That was first thing he'd noticed seeing her again. He stopped on the shoulder for the fifth time since starting down the road, trying to give his now bum left leg another rest. Bent over, wind pushing hard across the prairie and right up into him, he mumbled a question out loud. "What the fuck am I doing back here?" He knew the answer. He knew the answers for there were many, none of which he particularly wanted to face. He righted himself, sticking a thumb out from his hand and walked on wondering if people picked up hitchhiking Indians. They hadn't twenty years ago and he doubted they did now.

CHAPTER TWELVE
Mandan, North Dakota (1947)

The sun rose in all its colorful plumage on the Missouri, which even in this wash of feathered purple, orange, and pink still appeared muddy. It always was. Karl sat on the bank. Behind him, in various stages of ruin, was his parents' old cabin. He and his brothers still owned the land, but didn't really use the place save for the odd rendezvous to discuss business. Karl often fantasized about fixing it up, selling his place in town, and moving out here full time. The fantasy included Marilyn by his side as his lawfully wedded wife. Hell, he could even see a couple of kids running around the property, helping dig the fire pit, fishing from the banks, splashing in the brown water that muddled onward in a slow flow beneath him. Lost in his daydream of a memory not yet made and probably not within reach, he failed to hear the car pulling up the weedy, almost hay-like covered gravel drive leading to the cabin. He wrenched his neck around only after he was startled by the slamming of two car doors. There stood Frank and Christoph—still dressed in their clothes from the day before as he himself was.

"You can stare at that river all day, it won't get any clearer."

Frank had a way of cutting through it all with his words. He'd always had a command of language, even when they were kids. He never uttered anything in hesitation or uncertainty. Karl had the language too—he was better read than anyone in town and even secretly dabbled in writing some poetry—but was not as willing to weaponize words the way Frank could and often did. Karl was shy by nature, having stuttered as a child, though he could channel Frank's bravado and rapier wit if business depended on it. But when it came to the ladies, Karl was no match for his older, silver-tongued devil of a brother. Frank had dated dozens of girls by the time high school was behind him. Karl, on the other hand, had not even dated one by the time he was handed his diploma. Christoph was undeniably handsome. He had never had a problem with women, had always had his pick of the lot and was a bachelor still by choice, not default. Frank was the only one married among them, but he was a philanderer of the highest order. His wife, Eleanor, was a spend thrift who drowned her sorrows over Frank's betrayals by buying every new gizmo that was being manufactured in the booming economy of post-war America. They even had a television set despite the fact the screen flickered with a test pattern for most of the day and steadily after midnight.

Christoph made his way to the back porch of the cabin and began poking through some of the old artifacts still gracing its rotting floorboards. Frank watched Christoph and waxed nostalgic for a moment.

"Remember putting that porch on, Karl? You were too young to help or remember, Christoph."

Karl pushed himself up, wiped the dirt from his palms and stood with his hands on his hips. He knew what was coming. Frank always offered a bit of convivial banter before launching into the business of the day.

"Well, how'd it go with Reddeer?"

"Fine."

"He'll do it, then?"

"Yes. A hundred after it's done and a case of beer."

"A case of beer?"

"I sweetened the pot, he was wavering."

"Like hell he was. He's a drunk. You could have offered him the hundred and a thimble of your piss after you'd had a few pops at the Elks and he would have bit," Frank huffed, then added, "That's coming out of your pocket, Karl, not mine."

"Let's see if he even does it. If so, I'll make good, no worries, Frank."

"No worries? Nothing but worries, Karl, which is why I tell you what to do, not the other way around."

"What car will he use?"

"Figure it out," Frank blurted. Then turning to Christoph, "Stop poking around in all that old shit and start the car. I need a drink. The Elks should be open by now."

Karl started toward his vehicle, thinking it was an open invitation.

"Where do you think you're going?"

"The Elks."

"Not until you get that vehicle for your Injun buddy, you're not."

Christoph was behind the wheel now and Frank got in the passenger side. The Delahaye backed out and headed up the road, leaving a trail of Missouri River mud dust in its wake that drifted over and onto Karl, covering him in fine silt. He couldn't help but think it was fitting; he was always doing Frank's dirty work.

CHAPTER THIRTEEN
Williston, North Dakota (2011)

*

"Plant a thought, harvest an act, plant an act, harvest a habit, plant a habit, harvest a character, plant a character, harvest a destiny."
- Mandan Indian adage

*

Charlie wasn't sure how long he had been walking since leaving the parking lot at Cummins Energy and escaping Shannon's wrath, but now he stood in the bright light of a wide and cloudless Dakota sky outside the motel where he had spent the night with Dawes. He lit a cigarette and leaned against his own pick-up truck with its Florida plates that would have been a true anachronism twenty years before here in Williston, but which now was just another out-of-state plate among many from vehicles which had carried men, families, drillers, and dreamers to the area from the four corners of the United States and everywhere in between. Two weeks off without pay had put his own dreams for a leg up on hold, so he pondered his options, smoke from the cigarette curling around his head mimicking the fog inside his brain concerning just what to do next.

Charlie spotted Dawes' truck in the motel's recently-expanded parking lot, but had no intention of knocking on the door of Room 119. Dawes had been essentially homeless before the drilling boom and had readily signed up for the pro-rated accommodations arranged by Cummins Energy for their employees at every available hotel, motel, private home, and boarding room in town. New and nicer hotels had sprung up in what had always been farmland outside of Williston proper, but this fleabag suited Dawes just fine. "Just dirty enough to keep it interesting," as Dawes had told him the night before.

Charlie stubbed out the remains of his cigarette with a twist of his foot and turned to get into the truck, but stopped when he spotted Shannon's Torino parked at the far edge of the lot, but really in the grass. He looked around, but could not see her anywhere. He walked down toward the motel office, peered in through the window, but saw only the manager behind the counter reading the newspaper. The same donuts sat next to the coffee pot on the folding table near the flat screen TV, but there was no sign of Shannon. He lingered a moment thinking maybe she was using a restroom inside, but when the manager looked up at him with a glare, Charlie waved a little wave and made his way down the walk in front of the numbered room doors. He stopped in front of 119 and knocked.

There was a pause after he knocked on the door. Charlie could hear voices and then the door opened but only as far as the little chain on the other side of the door would allow. It was dark inside save for the TV flicker throwing random bursts of unnatural light here and there. Dawes was shirtless and his pants were unbuttoned and not quite up around his rail thin waist.

"Dude, what's up?" Dawes stuttered, his wild eyes maybe not admissible as evidence in a court of law, but circumstantial evidence of recent meth use nonetheless.

"I need to piss, let me in."

"I could use that piss. The other shit ended up back on the ground in the fucking parking lot," Dawes chortled back, then adding, "but I'm kind uh busy at the moment."

"Tell him to fuck off," Shannon's voice barked from somewhere inside the room.

Before anyone could speak again, Charlie lowered a shoulder and hit the door with enough force that the little gold chain barring entrance snapped in two, the force of the door swinging wide sending Dawes ass over ankles and onto the floor and its seedy, stained carpet.

Stepping inside, Charlie's eyes adjusted just enough to see that Shannon was naked on the bed he had slept in the night before, a needle, spoon and lighter on the bureau next to the bed.

"No worries. I'll fuck off. I just want my shit."

Charlie squinted his eyes still adjusting to the dark room and moved about the room stuffing a few personal items into his overnight bag he'd left behind that morning.

Dawes was back on his feet now and Shannon laughed uncontrollably, before stopping, taking a deep breath and invoking a tone bathed in contempt for Charlie. "This is my life, you son of a bitch, but you can fuck me too as long as you got some crank, cocaine, meth, or cash. If not, get... the fuck... out."

"Don't flatter yourself, junkie."

Dawes, not knowing quite what to do with his hands as they moved from his pants pockets to the front of his pale, undeveloped bare chest, tried to act as peacemaker with all the panache of the hyper high school dropout he was.

"Dude, there's enough pussy and powder in this room for both of us, come on sit down."

Charlie feigned a swing at Dawes who covered up like a skittish dog who was beaten regularly. Charlie glared at Shannon, her nudity more a nausea than an arousal, turned on his heel and stepped back out into the day's glare that seemed twice what it had before he had burst into the room. His head ached and he realized his hands were shaking badly as he made his way to his truck—leaving the parking lot with not a roar, but with a whimper, turning the truck gently onto Highway 1804 and proceeding well below the speed limit.

He had no intention of stopping at the 4 Mile Bar this time. He had no need for consumable courage. There was something raw and wild now raging within the blood-bathed cage of his heart. Twenty years of running away from his past had brought him to this moment. He glanced up at the rearview mirror to find his father's younger face in a wash of titian. Charlie contemplated the coming brisance about to shake the earth beneath the feet of two estranged men, about to shake the earth more than any drill driven two miles straight into the ground in search of tight pockets of trapped petroleum fortunes. Unlike the oil and gas, unaware of its own combustible potential, Charlie was well aware of his own. Charlie had been timid as a child, anxious as a teenager, and a volatile as an adult. The relationship with his father he had always hoped for had not transpired although there had still been riches to be mined if he had wished to: his father's fortune—money he had shunned, so had been denied. It was true, he couldn't correct a lifetime of mistakes in a day over even a decade back here among those who had been all but dead to him. But, he was beyond apologizing for his life and what it had done to other lives caught in its drifting, careless wake. He could, though, make sure at least Shannon had a shot at salvaging something from the seemingly soulless, shattered life she had fashioned in his absence. The more Charlie pondered it all, the more he realized he was wrong. He, in fact, needed a drink more than ever.

CHAPTER FOURTEEN
Bismarck, North Dakota (1947)

*

"That's how it is on this bitch of an earth."
- Samuel Beckett

*

John Paul Hoff cleared his throat. He stood behind a podium shoved into a corner of the Elks dining room. He picked up a glass of water sitting atop the notes of his prepared speech and walked out between the tables where fellow Elks were finishing a complimentary breakfast, a staple of the monthly meeting. He stopped in front of a table where four middle-aged white men in suits sat smoking, their plates of eggs, bacon, and hash browns in varying degrees of completion. He tipped the glass of water ninety degrees and a stream poured directly onto one of the plates, drowning the remnants of a breakfast. There was a collective gasp from the audience and the four men at the table, now splattered with watery grease droplets, were manically wiping their suit coats and trousers with cloth napkins.

"This, my fellow Elks, is what we are doing to thousands of acres of this great state: creating a mess in the name of supposed progress while ignoring the rights of thousands of Indians whose land we will expropriate to make it happen. Though this time we'll be generous and high-minded enough to offer them a check for their troubles. Have we learned nothing from this past century's indifference to our red-skinned brothers?"

"They're a bunch of damned ingrates living off government money anyway, what's the difference?" an Elk sitting at a back table shouted.

"And who created that situation, Dick? Was it the Mandan, the Arikara, the Hidatsa?"

A voice broke in from the vestibule of the club, "The weak shall not inherit the earth, John Paul, no matter what your bible says."

Frank Lund strode in through the proceedings, Christoph trailing behind with the usual smirk across his face.

"Who needs a drink? I'm buying," Frank announced as he made his way to the bar, a throng of Elks following his pied-piping.

John Paul Hoff, conceding this round to his young adversary, returned to the podium and stuffed papers into a briefcase as the majority of the Elks shouldered in against one another at the bar to take advantage of Frank's bribe disguised as lodge brother beneficence. Frank turned on a stool away from the bar, caught Hoff's eye as he closed the briefcase and winked at him as he raised his Gimlet in a mocking toast, then tipped it to his mouth, draining it before turning back to the bar and his confederacy of lushes.

CHAPTER FIFTEEN
Williston, North Dakota (2011)

Reporter Bob Mosier from the *Williston Herald* sat in a booth in the Lunch Box across from Cummins Energy's PR consultant, Roger Wharton. A waitress topped off the men's coffee cups, slid a check onto the table and walked away. Roger reached for the check, but Bob grabbed it before he could get to it.

"No offense, but it's not going to look real good if you're buying me breakfast, Roger."

"And it looks good for me if you're picking up the tab?"

"Dutch then, just give me a five and that'll keep us both from falling for a ten dollar bribe of overcooked eggs and weak coffee."

Roger fished a five dollar bill out of his wallet and then slid another five dollar bill under his coffee cup for a tip.

"I can't keep you from bribing the waitress, I guess. I'm a straight fifteen percent guy by nature."

"And by the constraints of the base salary for a prairie reporter."

Bob grinned and conceded, "Can't argue with that. But, back to the chemicals. We're talking benzene, toluene, xylene, and ethylbenzene just to name a few. Those alone make that fracking solution a highly toxic cocktail."

"The well testing results are on our side, Bob... for the most part."

"For the most part, but what about the ones that aren't?"

"You have health insurance?"

"I don't have a well, I have city water."

"That's not the point. If you've ever been screened for health insurance, you're more than familiar with the term 'pre-existing condition', no?"

"Aw, come on, that sounds as slippery as the flammable slurry they're finding in some of those well tests."

"Maybe so, but you have my quote for your article, so I suggest you use it verbatim. Cummins Energy is working not only within, but well within the letter of the law when it comes to their drill sites and has nothing but the health and welfare of the people of Williston and the rest of Western North Dakota in mind—not to mention what we're doing for the local economy.

"What about the folks downstream in neighboring states?"

"What about them?"

"What is Cummins' position on downstream pollution?"

"As far as Cummins Energy is concerned the Missouri stops at the border between North and South Dakota, Bob. They have no drill sites there or anywhere further south for that matter. The Missouri, Heart, and Knife Rivers and all the other tributaries here in North Dakota and Eastern Montana are all regularly tested and at a pretty penny to Cummins I might add."

Roger Wharton slid from the booth, reached back in for his folded suit jacket lying on the seat cushion, slipped it on and adjusted the knot of his tie.

"Pretty good first date, Bob. You're not easy, but by the looks of that dollar tip, you are cheap. Have a good day."

Roger walked on and out of the restaurant. Bob Mosier craned his neck to watch him walk down the sidewalk, then slid his dollar bill to Roger's side of the table and Roger's five dollar bill back to his, remarking under his breath, "Now who's the cheapskate?"

*

Karl Lund, nearing his eighty-ninth birthday, rubbed his eyes and placed his trifocals back upon the bridge of his nose. Before him, sitting on a TV tray—a permanent prop in front of his recliner in the TV room—was a thick legal document with little pink Post-It arrows pointing out where to sign.

"Do you need a break?"

The question came from the one of two men sitting on an old couch, the same two men who had been at Shannon's trailer the same morning to inform her that Mr. Lund was selling the rest of his substantial Williston-area land holdings to Cummins Energy, which included the five acres under her trailer. The two men from Cummins had made it a point not to go into detail when Mr. Lund had asked how the 'eviction' went. It had gone poorly; pure rage, thrown objects, and language that would have made a seasoned truck driver wince. The low point though was when she had offered them both sexual favors in return for another six months at the property. As it was she had thirty days to vacate the trailer which Cummins, not Mr. Lund, had offered to move for free to any available trailer park lot she could find to lease.

"No, I don't need a break. I want to sign before you bastards change your minds or lower the offer."

A slender and beautiful Hidatsa woman, Lana, entered the room carrying a small dish filled with pills and a glass of water, her long black hair trailing the curves of her that could have belonged to a twenty year-old, a woman half her age. The men from Cummins Energy gawked as they had when she had let them into the house.

"She's beautiful, isn't she, fellas?"

The North Dakota pale of the Cummins men's faces became a sudden glow of blush and they nodded simultaneously as their lips moved looking for words to deflect from the awkward moment flush with embarrassment and self-consciousness, but nothing came.

"He's so nice to me," Lana offered, filling the silence the two men were unable to.

"Well, that makes one person then," slipped from the Cummins Energy man nearest Karl.

There was a split second that hovered in the air between Karl and the Cummins men, hung there in a way which seemed to make the sitting room, already choked off from natural light by heavy curtains drawn across the windows, seem even darker.

"At least one of you hitmen speaks the truth," Karl conceded through a cough, snatching the deal breaker out of mid-air himself much to the relief of the two men seated on the couch. "Let's have a drink. Never completed a deal without a little pop. Join me."

"I don't think…," started the man closest to Karl before the other broke in.

"Of course, a toast of sorts."

Lana interrupted the less than festive proceedings, observing, "Knowing Mr. Lund's love for a deal, I'll offer one of my own. I'll mix the drinks, if Mr. Lund will take his pills."

"You should have had her make the deal for Cummins. You're overpaying by a heap," Karl chimed in, almost with a grin, and then motioned for it all to be so.

Lana placed the pills on the tray and Karl began to swallow them one at a time without benefit of beverage as Lana left the room to pour the drinks.

"She's Hidatsa. My brother Frank had a thing about Hidatsa women. You can see why."

The men from Cummins nodded, both anticipating a quick drink and an end to the near five years of crash and burn dealings they'd had with Karl Lund concerning the final pieces of the land puzzle in the Bakken Formation.

*

Just as three glasses of bourbon were being clinked together inside Karl Lund's sitting room, Charlie drove by outside on Highway 1804 without stopping. There was a voice not in his head, but in his heart that said, *Not yet*. Named for one of the years Lewis and Clark wandered the area, Highway 1804 was known as one of those scenic drives that really wasn't all that scenic. It was a flat, two lane stretch of blacktop which lulled a driver like a macadam hypnotist with little more than road whir and the white noise of compressing air through a partially opened driver-side window. It was now a cloudless, blue sky day with sunshine to spare and temperatures on the rise after the morning's heavy squalls back in Williston.

About fifteen miles east of Williston there was a turn-off for the Lewis & Clark State Park Campground. One night in a motel hell was enough for Charlie. Since leaving Williston unannounced twenty years ago, he'd always kept a tent and bed roll in any of the vehicles he'd owned. He had always preferred to sleep out under the stars. Plus, in this case it would provide some distance between the past and the present here in Williston as he pondered his future in this topography. He hoped that with nothing but wide open sky over his head, he would be able to think, to contemplate what was next. He'd spent his whole life trying to figure that out and the stars had not yet offered any answers, but they had also never asked any questions.

CHAPTER SIXTEEN
Mandan, North Dakota (1947)

Donald Reddeer woke with a sensation of sawdust in his mouth, the rumble of a locomotive in his head, but really in his ears. He'd spent the night on a bench outside the station and an early morning train from Minnesota had just pulled in carrying passengers from St. Paul. A motley crew of hung over Mandan and Hidatsa in traditional dress was stumbling around the platform in a faux war dance for the benefit of the passengers getting off in Mandan, hoping for a few coins for their efforts. Most of the disembarking passengers steered clear of the men in the well-worn war bonnets chanting and shuffling, still reeking of alcohol. Donald reeked as well and could not shake the dream he'd had, trying to chalk it up to the bottle from Karl that he had emptied before passing out on the bench. In the dream an eagle was flying across a vast body of water when it suddenly fell from the sky. He had plunged again and again into the water looking for the eagle without finding it, before finally waking to the sound of the train, shaking free at last from the drunken dreams which had stumbled around his inebriated sleep. Donald liked to believe that dreams were just dreams, not visions like his grandfathers had believed them to be. He never had nightmares.

Reality was nightmare enough and attested to yet again this morning by the chanting men whose withdrawal shakes were only masked by their exaggerated and clichéd native dancing. Annoyed, Donald rose unsteadily to his feet wondering where he could get a drink before having to drive all the way to Williston.

CHAPTER SEVENTEEN

Williston, North Dakota (1947)

Elsie Andersson hung laundry on the line. She sang an old
Mandan lullaby her mother had sung to her as a little girl. She
looked to her father, Harlan, the most beloved man in Williston. He
had an air about him, gentle but firm, and always fair. He'd worked
this land himself since taking over the old homestead for good after
he'd found his father swinging from a beam in the barn in the winter
of 1932; the economic depression sweeping the nation at the time
and the emotional depression which had driven the old man to drink
away his last few years having finally both been too much to bear.
There was no life in Williston that had not somehow been touched
by Harlan's generosity and kindness. He was now sixty and there
was a slight bend to his back from working the land all these years
though he was still at it with a vigor that shamed men half his age.
He was the single largest landowner in the area and worked most of
it himself, save for two seasonal hands out of Canada who came in
the spring and the fall. There were no sons, just Elsie.

Her mother, Little Crow, was a Mandan who had grown up on the
Berthold Reservation near Parshall, North Dakota. But unlike most
of the Indian women of Berthold, the reservation could not hold her.

She struck out on her own after high school, even worked for a lawyer in Minot for a stretch before lighting out for Mexico where she married a bullfighter whose luck in the ring simply ran out one day. She returned to North Dakota, stopping over in Williston en route to the reservation at Parshall and her family. But she never made it, instead meeting Harlan in less than ideal circumstances in the unpaved streets of Williston circa 1921. His team of horses, pulling a hay cart, spooked by a passing motor car, had lurched out into the dusty street, knocking her to the ground and breaking her leg in two places. Whether out of a sense of guilt, responsibility, or compassion, it was at Harlan's insistence that she stay at the homestead while recovering. Fate turned to love guaranteeing her journey home would end in Williston and they were married in 1925. Elsie came along in 1928, just a year before the stock market crash of 1929, but her mother died in 1934 from tuberculosis. In the thirteen years since his wife had passed, Harlan had not only run the farm, expanding its acreage by ten fold, but had raised Elsie singlehandedly. He had wanted her to go to college, but for now she was putting it off, so she could help out on the farm.

Elsie was a "half-breed" as some of the less than kind local folk had always and still tended to remind her. But their cruelty had hardened her and her resolve to help ensure the success of her father's farm. Self-pity was subjugated by the sense of pride she took in her father's accomplishments, her own and her half white, half red heart. She had the best of both her parents inside her and the few friends she let get close to her were the first to say that not only was she smart and strong, but a stunning beauty, just like her mother had been. Her father had never called her mother Little Crow, using Sarah instead, but Elsie always thought of her as Little Crow and wished she had been given an Indian name as well. But she had, though her father had never said as much. Elsie was chosen specifically because it had mimicked her mother's initials – 'L' and 'C' for Little Crow.

Everyone, it seemed, suddenly wanted her father's land. Any number of would-be buyers and potential lessees had stopped by over the past year. There was talk that there was oil under the land. It was hard to imagine as she watched the endless waves of wheat that spread across it to the horizon. Her father had even chased off one particularly persistent fella with a shotgun. The man was as persistent as he was handsome. She blushed thinking about him and wondered where the breeze had gone for her face was now ablaze. But the breeze was in fact still blowing and she danced a little dance with the empty laundry basket and hummed the melody to the little lullaby forever stuck in her head.

Harlan looked up from his work and back toward the house where he saw his now grown daughter dancing in between the laundry she'd finished hanging out to dry. *What will become of her?* He wouldn't be around forever to look after her.

CHAPTER EIGHTEEN
Williston, North Dakota (2011)

The two men from Cummins Energy had completed a deal for
Karl Lund's land, but they couldn't close the deal completely as Karl
had not quit talking since the first drinks had been served. He had
been going on and on about the old days. He had spoken lovingly
about his wife, Elsie, though he was emphatic, if contradictory, when
he told them he hadn't really loved her at all. But when the subject
of his only child being back in town came up, Karl's tone changed
radically as he railed about his wayward middle-aged son and how,
the fact of it was, he had really been an accident, had come late in
their lives.

"The first twenty years in the sack together never even grazed the
target, much less hit the bullseye."

They were all on their third bourbons now and finally the
Cummins men rose unsteadily, at last acting on a series of stolen
glances back and forth between the two over the past half hour.

"Where the hell are you two going?"

"We've got to get back," one of the men explained.

"So you can start punchin' holes in all that land, I suppose."

The Cummins men had started gathering the paperwork when a loud knocking came at the door out in the vestibule and continued without pause. Lana appeared in the vestibule, coming out of the kitchen after hearing the knocking, which had by this time become almost violent. If the prodigal son was about to return for the first time in twenty years, the Cummins men didn't want to be in the middle of a potential family fracas. Who knew what might jeopardize the deal—signed documents aside. All the same they stood frozen.

Lana looked to Karl as the pounding intensified.

"Get my god damn gun, Lana."

Lana shook her head from side to side in response to Karl's request and let out a slight, but pronounced *tsk* that was inaudible beneath the pounding. She turned, unlocked, and opened the door with a jerk of her hand.

Shannon burst through, knocking Lana to the floor. She leapt into the sitting room as though thoroughly possessed, her eyes wild with the fire of a few hours' meth binge. She paused a moment, visibly shaking, and then made a maniacal dash toward Karl.

"I'll kill you, you fucking old bastard…"

But then the men from Cummins were on her, wrestling her to the floor, furniture in motion amidst the melee and banging into and against walls and the floor. Karl, in a moment of pure adrenaline got to his feet more quickly than he had in a decade, grabbing his cane and hobbling toward the pile of flesh, ending up over her twisting, flexing figure held barely at bay by a choke hold administered by one of the Cummins men, the other stretched out across Shannon's legs as they continued to jolt and writhe beneath his substantial weight.

"I'll kill you first, you whore," sputtered Karl, spittle dripping from his bourbon-lubed lips. Karl raised the cane over his head, but at its apex he found himself in an unbreakable bear hug, not courtesy of Lana, but of a powerfully built, young man who had come out of nowhere into the room. The man, with a face which held a mix of Caucasian and Native American features seemingly unable to reconcile itself between the two, pulled Karl back to his recliner and eased him down into it.

"You'll give yourself a stroke. Now take it easy. I'll take care of this mess."

Dressed in jeans and a sweater which clung to his muscular arms, chest, and torso, he made his way over to the men holding down Shannon. He looked at Lana, taking control of the situation.

"Lana, call the police."

Then, casting his gaze to the floor, he reached down, seeming to simply sweep away the men holding Shannon, and with a powerful hand grabbed her by a shoulder and pulled her to her feet. He put his face close to hers and in terse, measured words queried her, "Why do you continue to fuck with my life?"

Sarcasm oozed from Shannon's lips as she offered with a twisted, little laugh, "Mommy knows best, Benjamin."

CHAPTER NINETEEN
Bismarck, North Dakota (1947)

"It's become a dog eat dog world, Christoph. That's just how it is."

Frank was feeling good, the drinks were going down, the crowd of Elks was thinning out and he and Christoph had retired to their usual booth. Nobody sat anywhere near them. No one ever did if they could help it.

John Paul Hoff wandered back into the club. He'd forgotten his hat in the chaos of the meeting's quick dissolution.

He reached beneath the podium, grabbed it, and placed it on his head, not noticing Frank was watching him.

"John Paul, come, sit. Have a drink with me."

John Paul walked toward the booth, the remaining Elk members' eyes upon him. No one was sure what was going to happen. Neither John Paul nor Frank were men to be trifled with. John Paul landed in front of Frank's booth.

"I think I will have drink."

John Paul removed his hat, set it on the table between Christoph's drink and Frank's, turned and pulled a chair from the empty table behind him, joining them at the booth.

Christoph, who was only twenty-one, no longer had the usual grin on his face.

"Should I leave?" Christoph asked nervously.

"Leave? Why in hell would you leave? John Paul is our friend. Isn't that right, John Paul?"

"We are two heads upon the same beast," he said calmly, his accent more evident than it had been during the meeting.

Frank motioned to the bartender for a round of drinks.

"Yes, John Paul, precisely, a two-headed beast," Frank concurred, but added, "Though I have decided to bite your head off. The beast can no longer move in opposite directions."

"True. And I will grant you that I probably won't get my way with the dam project, not with General Pick and his plan for flood control wooing every farmer from here to the delta." Then adding, "They're going to name a town after him I hear."

"Let me guess, Pick City?"

"Yes, why that's it," John Paul corroborated, a bit surprised Frank knew.

"I suggested it to the General last month. We had dinner in Rapid City," adding under his breath, "You know, the General's got quite a thing for the young ladies." The drinks arrived, all three men nodding in turn as each was placed in front of him.

Frank continued, "You see J.P., I have my connections in Washington as well."

"It's clear you are just another fist in a long line of fists at the end of the arm known as Manifest Destiny, readily available in this case to give the Indians in this state one last black eye."

"This coming from a man whose own people exterminated millions of Jews all over Europe," Frank shot back.

"I believe the puppet regime of Vidkun Quisling installed by Herr Hitler was fairly efficient at rounding up the Jews in your Norway," John Paul countered.

Frank raised his glass in a gesture of a toast, acknowledging and almost admiring John Paul's deft verbal swordplay.

"Here's to the Swiss, who at least were smart enough to act as an auction house and keep themselves in the black the whole time."

"Speaking of staying in the black and General Pick, there's going to be an investigation as to how the contracts are being handed out for work at the dam and I have a feeling when it's over your cement contract will be null and void. But you probably knew that seeing as you have your own connections in Washington."

John Paul stood, picked up his hat; his untouched glass upon the table in disrespectful juxtaposition to Frank's still hanging awkwardly in the air.

"And do me a favor, Frank, tell your brother Karl to stop parking outside my house waiting for Marilyn to slip into her night clothes."

John Paul placed his hat on his head and walked out before Frank could offer his own final volley.

Frank slammed the glass on the table, splattering himself and Christoph with bourbon.

Christoph wiped frantically at himself with his hands as Frank glared down into his empty glass, before exploding with, "Fucking... god... damned... Karl," and finishing by throwing the glass so that Christoph ducked though it was only vaguely in his direction.

CHAPTER TWENTY
Williston, North Dakota (2011)

Charlie had spent the better part of his adult life running away from those who would offer a hand, encouragement, an embrace—a chance. Here he was, back in his hometown and again he found himself on the outside by his own choice. It was time to shake things up—not for others, but for himself. After paying for his space at the Lewis & Clark State Park Campground, he'd gotten back into his truck and had headed west this time on Highway 1804, back toward a father he still feared, but really just an old man. He wasn't sure what he wanted from his father, but it wasn't money. What he wanted, really, but couldn't admit, was one honest conversation with the man who had been a mystery to Charlie his whole life. If he could know something of substance about his father, something beyond the faded but still frightening watercolor impressions of a childhood spent in abject paternalist fear, then he might know something more of himself; even if only where the worst parts of his own nature, his own character came from. That, at least, would be a beginning, a foundation to build upon. He only hoped that the words he had recited to himself over the years in faux confrontation with his father would be at his command when they were at last face to face. The fact did not escape him, though, that poor devils were born every day to uncaring fathers. Charlie was nothing special and he knew it, but what he also knew was that it was high time he crawled out of his self-imposed purgatory.

Durum wheat flanked either side of the flat, straight highway without surprises which allowed Charlie to meditate upon the already practiced speech he had been fine tuning since the day he had left twenty years ago. The ten miles back to his father's home ticked away quickly, tenth-of-a mile markers closing a gap of two decades more quickly than yearning itself. The sky was still clear and blue, the sun trying to coax what really was already springtime from the ground. A feeling of warmth, of almost calm came over Charlie until he saw the lights—flashing reds and blues within a strobe of stuttering whites.

He eased the truck across the yellow line into the oncoming lane and then into the grass a few hundred feet from the front of his father's house. Charlie squinted through the windshield against the glare of the day. He could see a few North Dakota State troopers milling about, two men in suits, and a woman with her hands cuffed behind her back. Shannon. The curves of her body had been filed away somewhere in his animal brain, like a chalk outline of a murder victim who was somehow still alive. He'd been in town fewer than seventy-two hours and already all hell was breaking loose—or maybe, he thought, had been busting loose all along. Whichever, he was about to get knee deep in it as he got out of the truck and headed for the driveway where a shuffle of folks along with a shiver of ghosts waited.

It was only about thirty yards or so to the driveway which was still just a scatter of gravel all these years later. The wind picked up whirling dust, flinging it into his eyes. With each step a new memory seemed to blur his thoughts even further. Why had it been that he had never felt like a grown man in this town? He knew for the moment he had to hide the child walking along in his shadow and step into the world of adults and the shit they waded through on a daily basis. He cleared his throat and was about to speak with some authority—*What's going on here?* at the ready but disarmed by one of the state troopers barking right at him in a flat, militaristic tone, "Can I help you?"

Everyone was now staring at Charlie. He felt they all could see right through him, see the shell of a man he forever wandered around in. As usual, he stuttered in the presence of authority, within the pressure of conflict.

"Uh, yeah, um, uh, I know her."

"That wasn't the question," the officer snapped back, his holstered aggression palpable, then adding, "Identify yourself."

"He's my husband and he's an asshole," Shannon broke in.

The second trooper stepped up and took control, booming, "Everybody shut up, right now."

He turned square to Charlie, drawing his service revolver and pointing it flat at him.

"Get down on the ground, face down, hands behind your back, now."

Charlie started to speak in his own defense, but whatever words had begun to come out were lost to the scuffle of heels and the thud of his own body hitting the ground hard. With a state trooper on top of him with a knee in his back, Charlie was cuffed and yanked back to his feet before he knew what was happening.

Never known for her situational appropriateness, Shannon did not disappoint in this instance and laughed like a pathetic high school girl after getting high for the first time. Charlie's wallet was taken from his back pocket as he spit a mix of gravel, spittle, and blood from his mouth.

"Karl Charles Lund, Jr.," one of the troopers announced, then asking, "Karl Lund your father?"

"His name's Charlie, like Charlie Brown," Shannon managed through chortling snorts.

"Yes," Charlie answered, "He's my father. Can I ask what's going on here?"

The trooper holding his wallet wasn't ready to answer questions and had another of his own.

"You married to this woman?"

"Technically."

The trooper waved his wallet in his face, punctuating his words, "You either are, or you are not, which is it?"

"Yes, I am, sir."

The other trooper grabbed Charlie's hands and took the cuffs off and turned Charlie around to face him. Shannon was now chanting a cartoonish, faux Indian chant, mocking Charlie's Native American heritage.

"She should be charged with breaking and entering and aggravated assault," the trooper informed Charlie, "but your father is not pressing charges. She can't drive, though, her license is expired."

"I never touched the rotten, old son of bitch," Shannon spit.

"Get her out of here. Do you understand?"

Charlie shook his head in the affirmative to the officer.

"Un-cuff her."

Shannon continued to rant and Charlie was about to head for the truck when he noticed an Indian woman standing in the doorway of the house. Even at this distance, he could see she was beautiful and that she looked like she was Hidatsa. It wouldn't be all that shocking if his father were now remarried and even less shocking to a woman half his age. What would have shocked Charlie, though, was the fact that his father had never loved Charlie's mother—at all.

CHAPTER TWENTY-ONE
Mandan, North Dakota (1947)

*

"It is in the darkness of their eyes that men get lost"
- Black Elk

*

There was not a drink to be had anywhere. Donald had stumbled around, trying to gain entrance into some of the bars already open at this hour to accommodate the railyard workers just getting off the overnight. There seemed to be a particularly strong vehemence coming from the white townspeople this morning, but Donald was used to their disgust and derision and wanted only a little something to take the edge off. Behind the building that housed the butcher he found his little something. There, two Arikara teenagers were sipping out of cough medicine bottles. They sat on the ground and stopped talking as Donald landed in front of them. He simply motioned with his hand and was immediately in possession of both bottles. He drank what was left in both, wiping his mouth on his sleeve and then, almost politely handing back the empty bottles to them. They knew all too well Donald's reputation and had held their eyes to the ground during the entire exchange. Donald had broken many an arm by just grabbing and twisting with his powerful grip.

Donald walked away, his need to feel something other than his hung over soberness not even close to being sated. It was going to be a long day driving out to Williston and he thought of simply heading out of town to walk the Missouri where he could spend the day relieving others of their various intoxicants. But, the promise of big money from Karl Lund kept him on the hook, and he shuffled his way slowly to the meeting point at the east end of town, the sun's growing glare causing him to squint his bloodshot eyes into slits barely able to hold up the red, swollen lids sagging above.

Karl recognized Donald's large-framed shuffle from a quarter mile away. He could see how compromised Donald was this morning after the previous evening's beers at the Corner Bar and the bottle which had surely been imbibed afterward. The derelict army of Indians in the Mandan/Bismarck area was not above sniffing everything from Sterno to industrial cleaning products to keep themselves physically and mentally compromised and Karl was well aware of this fact and was already lamenting the fact that he would have to have Donald use his car for the trip to Williston, a brand new Packard Clipper Six he himself had only driven for a week. Nonetheless, he pulled alongside Donald and motioned for him to get in.

"Are you drunk?"

"I wish."

"Good, stay sober for the next twenty-four hours and I'll add another fifty to your payday."

Donald grunted, knowing it wouldn't be easy even with the added incentive.

"We'll head for the Elks. I'll get out there and then meet you at the cabin tomorrow morning. Say, eight?"

Donald knew the cabin well. The Lunds sometimes used it as a meeting place when they had business with him.

"Eight," Donald confirmed and then slumped down in the seat, closing his eyes.

Karl kept talking, going over details, but Donald heard little if any of it. He knew what he was supposed to do. His spirit was already down the road; job done, a full bottle in hand, a pocket full of cash and easy street for the long Dakota winter everyone knew was coming. It always did.

*

Marilyn Hoff walked out into an autumn morning as fresh as any she could remember. She had come to pray at the Church of Saint Joseph every day since her mother had been taken to North Dakota State Hospital in Jamestown. The fact was her mother had not been taken away, but driven there by her father. Marilyn never really remembered a time while she was growing up that she had not thought of her mother as peculiar, at least compared to the mothers of her friends. Not that Marilyn had had all that many friends—then or now for that matter. She herself was odd and she recognized this. *Was that the difference between thinking you were crazy and actually being crazy?* She had her mother's facial features, her slender figure, and her tendency to get lost in a world of make-

believe or "nonsense that would add up to nothing," as John Paul
Hoff had told his wife years before and now told Marilyn.

As the only child of a man who most saw as gruff, but who was
more doting than anyone in Mandan would ever have imagined, her
whimsies had been indulged. When as a teenager she had wanted to
paint, he'd mail ordered her all the supplies necessary to do it right
from an art supply store in New York City. When she had wanted to
skip school, he would initially forbid it in front of her mother then
secretly show up driving behind her in the old Buick as she walked
to school, pull alongside and open the door for her to get in; a day of
hooky spent in the big department store in Bismarck or at the
movies. He had spoiled her rotten most likely as way to compensate
for her mother's often erratic behavior; behavior that became even
more erratic after Marilyn's brother died in the war. By the time
Marilyn was in high school, her mother was drinking heavily at
home and although her father tried to hide the fact, many nights she
lay in bed listening to their fights about it. The final straw had come
last autumn, when her father received a call from the police to
inform him that Mrs. Hoff had been picked up and taken to the
lockup after a beat cop had seen her walking down the train platform
without her clothes on. Marilyn worried such a time bomb was
waiting for her, waiting inside her mind, a mind that she was well
aware was prone to flights of fancy and a gnawing sensation she had
once tried to describe to a school nurse. The nurse had told her the
'gnawing sensation' in her brain was nothing unusual, was
something all women felt from the long carried guilt of original sin.
At twenty-one, Marilyn was still a virgin and still unmarried, neither

condition that unusual for a young woman in the Midwest in the late 1940's, but conditions she had been considering rectifying and she knew just the man for both jobs. Their pre-arranged 'date' would be tonight.

*

"Where is everybody?"

Karl looked around the empty Elks Lodge, spying only Frank in the usual booth and the barkeep who was leaning on the bar over a newspaper he was reading. Karl had entered in a good mood, but quickly became aware that it wouldn't last long.

"Where's Christoph? I thought he was here with you."

Frank followed Karl with his eyes until he landed in front of him at the booth, never uttering a word in response to Karl's inquiries, before commanding, "Get the car, Karl," as he pushed the keys away from himself on the table top and not stopping until they teetered over the edge.

"I just got here. Don't you want to know how it's going?"

"How it's going? How what's going?

"You know, the job we have Donald doing."

The last word had barely left Karl's mouth when Frank reached up and grabbed Karl's necktie, jerking his head down to the table where it now rested. Karl's eyes were wide and he gasped a bit as Frank twisted the necktie in his balled fist. Frank leaned in, his lips so close to Karl's ear that Karl could feel the warmth of his bourbon breath as he whispered in measured words, "Don't... ever... mention... Reddeer... or... any... fucking... job... ever... in...

this… fucking… place… again. Now go get the fucking car. I need some action."

"Drive yourself."

"What the fuck did you say?"

Karl was wondering the same thing, he'd never spoken to Frank like that.

"I… uh, I have a date."

As if on cue, Christoph entered the Elks, a woman on his arm, both laughing while pawing at one another. It gave Frank time to think and he waved Christoph toward the bar.

In that moment the angle came to him and Frank softened his tone, knowing he was holding all the cards with his question, "Hoff's daughter?"

"How do you know that?"

"Hoff was just here, he told me to tell you to stay the hell away from her."

Karl felt uneasy, not about Hoff, but about Frank knowing so much.

"What time, lover boy?"

"What?"

"The date?"

"Six."

Frank played his hand, knowing he had Karl beat as usual.

"I'll have you back in time and I'll tell you what, you can show me that new car of yours. Just drop me off back here before you head over to Mandan to meet with what's her name."

Karl leaned in, whispering, "Reddeer has my car."

"No problem. Mine's across the street. You can use it—pick up your filly in style. I'll catch a ride home with Christoph tonight after you and I get back from Stanton."

"Why not just have Christoph drive you now?"

"I got him doing a little job for me while we're gone. I know how you don't like hittin' anybody."

Karl was visibly uncomfortable, but Frank had him, as usual, in a corner, and as usual it was easier to go along to get along especially if it meant he wouldn't have to break his date with Marilyn. She had asked to see him which was unusual, had even asked him to pick her up which meant her father wouldn't be around. It was adolescent of him to think this, but maybe she wanted to elope. He'd asked her before, to just head for the Black Hills, get hitched in Rapid City and maybe never come back.

Frank dangled the keys in front of Karl's face.

"Hey, Casanova, go start the car. I'll be out after I talk to Christoph."

Karl's daydream collapsed and he grabbed the keys, headed for the door, thinking, *The sooner this is over, the better.*

*

The car moved back and forth across the center line and wasn't so much being driven by Donald Reddeer as it was being herded; herded by a red-skinned cowhand, punch-drunk not from too many days in the saddle, but from the all too sober reality of more than ten hours since his last real drink. The glaring sun across the windshield was like a cinematic version of a headache that mixed none too well with the blur of macadam rolling out ahead which was creating a sort of slow-motion nausea in his stomach despite his best efforts to keep his speed up. He just wanted to arrive in Williston and get out of the car, preferably at a bar first. A few pops would be necessary to steady his hands for the task at hand. *Hurt him real bad, real bad, but don't kill him.* Donald knew how to do his job. If Karl had repeated the instructions one more time, Donald might have turned his knuckles on him. White people had a habit of talking to Indians as if they were all completely stupid, without a thought of their own in their heads. *Drunk ain't the same as dumb.* He would enjoy beating the hell out of this white man when he finally arrived—*Any white man.* He'd been instructed not to hurt the daughter, but as he drove on it wasn't hurting her that entered his mind. For the moment, his rage and lust supplanted his need for a drink and he pushed the accelerator closer to the floor and drove straight down the road, perfectly between the shoulder and the center line at last.

*

"Punch it, Karl. You drive like a woman."

Frank was right. Karl realized if he had any chance of making it back for his date with Marilyn, he'd better step on it. And so he did.

"That's more like it, brother. Now, tell me about you and Hoff's daughter?"

"What about it?" Karl asked, feigning ignorance.

"Let me rephrase my question. Are you rolling in the hay with her yet? I admit she's pretty for a white woman. Is she treating you good?"

"It's not like that."

"What's it like then, Karl? We got time. Tell me, what's it like then?"

"I love her," Karl answered bluntly, surprising himself and Frank.

"Love? What the hell does that mean?"

"It's the opposite of what you feel toward women, especially…," Karl answered before trailing off.

"Especially who, my wife? Bingo. And once again I gotta finish what you start. Listen, Karl, love is for saps and guys who can only put two dimes together, but always wish they had a quarter."

"So, you've *never* been in love, Frank?"

"Plenty, but only about twenty minutes at a time."

Karl drove faster now, knowing the sooner he got Frank to his Hidatsa mistress, the sooner those twenty minutes would be up and he could get back down to Marilyn.

"It could be advantageous, you know," Karl planted as a way of killing time.

"Yeah, imagine that poor son of bitch Hoff havin' to watch his daughter walk down the aisle with a Lund brother," Frank volleyed back, taking the bait.

"He'd have a god damned heart attack right there in the church."

"I'd enjoy seein' that. We'd better put Christoph on it though. He's a real looker. I mean, what the hell does she see in you?"

It took Karl everything not to jam on the brakes and send Frank through the windshield, but Karl could play along too. "Nothing, I suppose."

"Ah, hell, go for it. Christoph likes them much younger than that anyway. We all got our burdens, I suppose."

And Frank's burden was his own ego. He couldn't just destroy and humiliate a culture that had been marginalized and brutalized, herded into submission on reservations not fit for animals. No. Frank felt the need for absolute power over the Three Affiliated Tribes and he did this by indiscriminately bedding down with any gal with Native blood he could bribe. Soon, even their reservations would be sacrificed, submerged, and stolen from them and all of it to the benefit of his older brother. All this passed through Karl's mind as he drove on, his eyes moist and his mind a tangle of allegiances which were being torn apart in a way Frank would never understand, much less condone.

*

"The members of the tribal council sign this contract with heavy hearts. Right now, the future does not look good to us."
- George Gillette, Tribal Chairman for Three Affiliated Tribes (1948)

*

The agreements between Washington, D.C. and what would become the Three Affiliated Tribes had always been defined by the U.S. government's avarice. The Pick-Sloan Missouri River flood plan passed by Congress in 1944 and authorizing six dams on the upper Missouri, including the Garrison Dam, was no different. Indifference, as a matter of course, was what had always ruled the day when it came to the agreements between Washington and the tribes of the Great Plains, including the Mandan, Hidatsa, and Arikara. The first of these, the Fort Laramie Treaty of 1851, was procured by treaty commissioners from these three plains tribes, along with the Arapaho, Assiniboine, Cheyenne, and Sioux, to, in essence, provide safe passage through these traditional tribal lands for the ever increasing streams of emigrants, immigrants, and especially prospectors. In 1848, at Sutter's Mill in Coloma, California, on the American River in the Sierra Nevada mountain range, James Marshall picked out pieces of lustrous metal from a water wheel for a mill he was helping to construct for John Sutter and over the next eight years some 300,000 people flocked to Northern California in search of gold. Nearly a quarter million of these hopeful souls came across land from the east and so through the traditional lands of many Native American tribes, including those of the Plains Indians. The Fort Laramie Treaty of 1851 was, in its essence, a treaty designed to guarantee, as best as the U.S. government could, safe passage for this flood of humanity across the Kansas and Dakota Territories on their way to pick up the California Trail, beginning just west of the Missouri River and continuing on some 2000 miles to the gold fields of California—which ironically became part of the United States just a few weeks after the discovery at Sutter's Mill with the signing of the Treaty of Guadalupe Hidalgo through which Mexico relinquished its claim to the territory after losing the Mexican-American War. With the signing of this treaty by all of the affected tribes save for the Crow, a mixture of Manifest Destiny and gold fever was already conspiring against tribes like the Mandan, Hidatsa, and Arikara to impinge upon the lands they had occupied for over a millennium. It might go without saying given the 20-20 hindsight concerning Washington's dealings with Native Americans, but the promised compensation for the tribes to hold up their end of the deal for this treaty was not only reduced before it was completed, but was for the most part sparingly, if at all in some cases, paid.

Federal recognition of the ancestral lands of the Mandan, Hidatsa, and Arikara came with the treaty of 1851, but it was a hollow victory for what would become the Three Affiliated Tribes. Those emigrating west didn't always make it to California and so the increased presence of whites in the Dakota Territories not only brought conflict, but the inevitability of Washington's increasing activity on tribal lands across the Great Plains. The foothold for this activity had also been established by this first Laramie Treaty, as it contained a proviso which allowed the U.S. Army to establish forts throughout the Missouri River Valley, forts that would later become the launching pads for campaigns against the tribes of the Great Plains and quasi-feudal outposts of the reservations which would be established throughout the region over the next fifty years.

The next seventeen years following the treaty of 1851 were further defined by warring, skirmish, and broken promises between the U.S. Army and Plains Indians, the Sioux Nation the most defiant among them. With the conclusion of the Civil War, Washington turned its eye to the territories of Kansas and the Dakotas and the former Union Army was tasked with bringing this area of the reunified country under control. The second Treaty of Fort Laramie, or Sioux Treaty as it was also known, came in 1868 and was an agreement between the Arapaho, the Yanktonai Dakota, and three bands of the Lakota which was made up of seven different Sioux tribes. Essentially another land grab by Washington, it did concede the Black Hills region to the Lakota, promising them ownership of this traditional hunting ground. But gold defined the future of the agreement as it did in many others that were made then broken. The influx of prospectors in the 1870's, spurred on by a supposed gold boom in these sacred Lakota lands, which was more a bust when all was said and done, was the ultimate undoing of the agreement as Lakota and Northern Cheyenne attacked these interlopers. The grim fate of General Custer and his forces at the Battle of the Little Big Horn while on a detail to round up a renegade band of Sioux in June of 1876, only further fanned the flames of this conflict and the ire of Washington, leading to the Black Hills War or Great Sioux War of 1876-1877 and the ultimate seizure of the Black Hills by the U.S. Government at its conclusion.

The time period also marked the Centennial Exposition in Philadelphia celebrating the hundredth anniversary of the signing of the Declaration of Independence. There, Alexander Graham Bell displayed his telephone along with ketchup from Heinz, Remington's typewriter, and Charles Elmer Hires' root beer. The future of the country was at hand, the Industrial Revolution had transformed not only the country, but the world over the past one hundred years and in its wake indigenous populations everywhere became further and further marginalized. The Three Affiliated Tribes were no exception. Relegated to the Fort Berthold Reservation by the original Fort Laramie treaty of 1851, which provided some 12 million acres, The Arikara, Hidatsa, and Mandan tribes looked on in vain over the next forty years as a series of acts by Congress and executive orders reduced its area to less than 1 million acres total. By the time Secretary of Interior A. J. Krug approved the appropriation of an additional 150,000 plus acres of reservation land for the Garrison Dam project in early 1948, it was easy to understand why the photo of the signing ceremony captured George Gillette, hereditary chief of the Mandan and chairman of the Affiliated Tribes, with a hand over his eyes, crying.

*

Tribal Chairman Gillette's tears during the signing of the Garrison Dam agreement were still a few months off in the autumn of 1947, but the wheels were well in motion and all of the players, including John Hoff and the Lund brothers knew it. Frank Lund, along with brothers Karl and Christoph, had inherited a middling cement operation that had included about twenty employees and four trucks when their father, Gunnar Lund, died from a sudden heart attack two years before. Since then, through Frank's dogged determination, unrelenting will, and iron fist business practices, the company had become one of the main suppliers of cement for the increasing post-war road, construction, and industrial projects popping up all over North Dakota. The state was still overwhelmingly rural by eastern standards circa 1947, but therein lay the opportunities and Frank was not about to let anyone or anything get in the way of the potential windfall waiting in the wings and along the banks of the Missouri River. The Garrison Dam and the other dams proposed for the Missouri within the Pick-Sloan Plan would not only bring hydro-electric power, flood control, and a much needed irrigation system to farmers all along the river, but a financial boon to any business or businessman fortunate or connected enough to get in on the spoils. After all, the government would be footing the bill and the government had a reputation and a tendency to overpay while not overseeing very carefully exactly what it was they were paying for. But Frank Lund had always been looking beyond the immediate and had already been hatching his next move in a state that many around the country saw as an afterthought full of Indians and dirt farmers. There were, in fact, plenty of both, but there was also a unique geology to the area that belied the flat, face value of a state known more for its annual snowfall amounts than its natural resources in late 1947.

CHAPTER TWENTY-TWO
Stanton, North Dakota (1947)

Karl, inconveniently tasked with chauffeuring his big brother,
pulled Frank's Delahaye 135 convertible into Stanton—a ramshackle
of a town founded in 1883, but only incorporated as a city earlier in
the year. The roads were unpaved and Frank daydreamed that Lund
Cement would have a hand in bringing Stanton into the future. The
reality was the streets would remain unpaved until 1966 and the
future just another specter in a town full of ghosts from the past, like
that of Sakakawea, or Sacagawea as grade school students learning
about the Lewis and Clark Expedition called this Lemhi Shoshone
woman. Stanton, located on the banks of the Knife River, had been
home to a number of Hidatsa villages and there were still
indentations from their very un-Native American earthlodges which
had one hundred and fifty years earlier comprised several villages
including Sakakawea's village of Awatixa. Small pox and white
settlement eventually sealed the fate of Hidatsa villages, but at the
time Lewis and Clark came to this area in 1804, they were a part of a
thriving community which would become historically significant as
the location where the explorers met Sakakawea, who joined the
expedition as an interpreter and traveled with them to the Pacific

Ocean before returning to the area in 1806, two years and thousands of miles later.

Frank cared little for the history of the area. His only connection to the geography he now rambled through was his twice monthly pilgrimages to the area for pleasures of the flesh. He would have tried to bed Sakakawea if she'd been a Hidatsa for he had a penchant for the women of this tribe, especially the ones he could buy for two dollars an hour at a rundown Victorian style home on the edge of town. The brothel had a small selection of Arikara and Mandan women, but only one Hidatsa. He didn't know her name, never asked, didn't want to know. Names only created inhibitions and his wife, whose name he never spoke in public, was full of them, which is why Frank went elsewhere for his manly needs and particular fetishes. Karl was all too aware of these fetishes and was at Frank's beck and call when these urges to take to the road in search of the pleasures of a Hidatsa woman's flesh hit. Karl always waited in the car, tried to sleep until Frank emerged looking for a steak dinner, a good cigar, and a few stiff drinks, and did his best to ignore the abject squalor of the small rundown towns and dismal reservations where Frank found his cheap thrills. And so, just as the many times before, he slept as Frank did his business.

Karl awoke to the wrapping of a small fist on the car window. He wasn't sure how long he had been asleep, but as his eyes found their focus, the figure of an Indian woman, her blouse pulled open, her breasts shaking back and forth, greeted him. Adrenaline replaced the slow blood of sleep in his veins and he opened the car door with such force and swiftness that it knocked the poor woman to the ground.

"What the fuck's wrong with you, Karl? I know she's just a squaw, but hell, you usually gotta give them the two dollars first before they'll get on their backs like that."

Frank chortled and appeared from the rear end of the car, his Hidatsa trick on his arm.

"Come on, start the car. We're all gonna take a ride and get a bottle," Frank ordered.

Karl tried to help the Indian woman to her feet out of a sense of responsibility, but his anger escaped and he dropped her back to the ground as he spat at Frank, "You've had your fun. We're leaving."

The skin of Frank's face seemed to droop an inch as he set his dead eyes on Karl. There was a split second of pure silence which seemed to be followed immediately by the loudest cricket chatter Karl had ever heard and his own staccato breathing. And then there was a gun in Frank's hand at the end of his leveled right arm, the most seemingly natural extension of a body one could imagine.

CHAPTER TWENTY-THREE
Williston, North Dakota (2011)

"I would have killed him," muttered Shannon in between dabbing again and again at the blood still leeching through her split lip.

Charlie rolled his eyes without rolling his eyes as he lit a cigarette and handed it to her. She took it without looking at him and dragged hard on it, holding it a moment in her lungs and then exhaling a rolling grey cloud across the inside of the front windshield.

"What do you care? You'll make out alright. I can only imagine how much they paid him for all that land."

"What land? Your land?"

"No, his whole stinking spread."

Charlie jerked the wheel of the truck, sending the car to the shoulder in a shudder of gravel spray, breaking hard to stop the vehicle.

"All the land? He sold all the land? To Cummins?"

"The same creeps who told me I had thirty days to get out of the trailer."

Charlie dropped the truck into drive and banged a u-turn almost before the last word had left Shannon's mouth.

"Come to think of it, the old man will probably stiff you since he's always hated you, but Benjamin ought to make a pretty penny. He's quite the grandpa's boy these days," Shannon baited.

"How is he?"

"That's the best you can do twenty years after abandoning the two of us?"

Shannon's face was hidden from him and all he could see was her long, tangled mane as he gave a glance her way. Though he could not see it, there was now a knowing grin on Shannon's face as she breathed purposefully upon the window and drew little dollar signs in the condensation spreading across the window. There was about to be one hell of a family reunion. Fireworks in April.

"This will sound fucked up, but I'd like to see him. If he'd want to see me that is."

Shannon drew a smiley face near the dollar signs and answered, "Doubt it…," adding under her breath, "… but he will."

CHAPTER TWENTY-FOUR
Somewhere between Mandan and Williston, ND (1947)

Donald was raw. His frayed nerves no longer had any control over his shaking hands and even he was surprised, as he turned around from relieving himself on the side of the road, how wild his eyes looked in the reflection of his face in the car window. He walked along the side of the car, unplugged the gas cap and leaned his large frame over until his nose was flush against the opening and took a series of long inhalations. His head became cloudy and he lifted it to the sky until his eyes landed upon a vulture perched atop a utility pole which spread its wings and lifted from its perch, swooping so quickly and close to his head that he ducked and flinched in one motion as the scavenger landed atop the roof of the car, spooking Donald. This was surely a sign and not a good one and in this moment as the vulture moved its wings as if to menace him further, Donald raised a clenched fist and dropped it with a resounding *thud* upon the roof, sending the bad omen back into the air, its black leafed wings beating with purpose as it flew on up the road.

Donald's head was no longer in the clouds from his ephemeral, gasoline fume intoxication. His hands had stopped shaking, but the rest of his body shook as though a series of chills had suddenly gripped him. He could feel the goose bumps across his flesh and he considered hawking the car, pocketing the minimal gas money Karl had given him, and striking out away from this life that had become not much more than a slumped shadow limping along toward death. He had always wanted to go to California. He had never seen the ocean. He wanted to see the ocean. And if he couldn't reinvent himself in a place full of sunshine and movie stars with bodies so tanned they could pass for family, then he thought he would simply wade into the ocean until he could no longer walk; give himself to the spirit of the Great Sea, for here in this desert of wheat he was already slowly drowning and he knew it. But Donald Reddeer knew if he hawked the car, he would most likely get no further than Montana and the bars that spotted the straight, flat roads between where he stood and the state line. He would drink the equivalent of the resale price of a brand new automobile and be right back where he had always found himself standing: in the middle of a landscape more desolate than the mind could ever grasp, but somehow understanding the geography inside him was what truly made it so foreboding and unforgiving.

CHAPTER TWENTY-FIVE

Stanton, North Dakota (1947)

Frank's eyes had gone hollow and dark crescents hung in the droop of the skin beneath them. Frank was only a few years older, but Karl felt as though he had just watched him age a decade. Frank did not speak, which was far worse than when he did which was hard for anyone who had ever been on the receiving end of one of his tirades to imagine. The two Indian women cowering behind Frank began to move away from the scene and without seeing them do so or turning to look at them, Frank spit, tight-lipped, an order for them to, "Stay the fuck put." They did, not knowing whether Frank was talking to Karl or to them, but not taking any chances.

Frank began to laugh, but there was nothing even remotely funny about the current standoff. His laughing only made him appear that much more unhinged.

"Big date there, little brother? Afraid you're gonna miss out on some action with Hoff's daughter?"

Karl called his bluff, thinking *He's not going to shoot me*, and turned to toward the car and took a step. Then behind him, *bang*, the gun went off.

Karl could feel the urine soaking into his slacks and dribbling down the insides of his legs. He felt an absence of air in his lungs and he looked to his chest to see if he'd been shot through the back. It was then he heard Frank's voice through the underwater ringing in his ears.

"We can head out, little brother, as soon as you change that flat."

In the late afternoon light the air took on a chill and Karl began to shiver in a way he couldn't shake. To be his own man, to make his own decisions, to decide what was right and good at any given moment was all he wanted anymore. It was then he thought of Donald Reddeer and realized he was as much a pawn in Frank's game as the Indian he had sent on an errand earlier in the day. He thought of going to John Paul Hoff with all he knew, but he was already in deep, but with no idea how much deeper he soon would be.

CHAPTER TWENTY-SIX
Williston, North Dakota (2011)

Charlie was barreling back east on Highway 1804 and was so lost in thought about his father's land and the events of the previous two days that he nearly missed the drive into the old homestead. His truck sprayed gravel into the lawn until it came to rest at an awkward angle in front of the house.

Inside, heated words were flying like buckshot back and forth between the Cummins men and Karl, who leaned his frail body forward toward the men, the old wooden cane in his hand the only thing keeping him upright.

"What do you mean? You signed the papers," one of the Cummins men shouted, all the civility of the previous hours now long gone.

'Sure 'nough, my John Hancock's all over that stack of toilet paper, but you'd be better off wiping your ass with it than taking it down to the deed office at the courthouse."

Stepping in between the parties, Benjamin held out his large palms in front of the warring factions and turned to Karl.

"What do you mean?"

"It ain't mine to give anymore. I signed it over a week ago to somebody else."

Benjamin squinted his eyes almost enough to release a smile from his poker face, one he was proud to have maintained since the day he had shown up nearly a year ago at his grandfather's after leaving home; the same trailer his mother called home and was being evicted from; the event which had precipitated the ugly scene he had broken up. It had been an ugly scene as long as he could remember. But now the spoils would go to him and he would stick them in everyone's face around Williston, a community which had nothing but contempt for him; a contempt which was rooted in a family history Karl had related to him over and over again and to which he had diligently feigned to listen to without interruption anticipating his loyalty might bring him to this moment—a moment where a cut of his grandfather's empire seemed within reach at last and maybe more than a cut, perhaps the whole shebang.

CHAPTER TWENTY-SEVEN

Somewhere between Mandan and Williston, ND (1947)

*

"You ask me to dig for stones! Shall I dig under her skin for bones? Then when I die I cannot enter her body to be born again." – Wovoka, Paiute spiritual leader

*

Off the side of the road, in a thrush of winter wheat, Donald Reddeer danced a ghost dance, around and around. When his feet finally came to a stop he dropped to his knees and mumbled prayers to the Great Spirit, asking for guidance, but mostly for deliverance. The vulture which had swooped down a half hour before, coming to rest atop the vehicle had spooked him badly. He knew it would take more than a few beers from a package store in Williston to shake the black cloud that had descended and so he had danced, hoping dead elders would protect him in the hours that remained between him and a payday that would keep him in stiff drink and cigarettes for the winter. The wind had begun to slice through the standing wheat encircling his man-made clearing. His face was warm from the constant motion of the past half hour, but he'd been on the prairie long enough to know when an early snow might be in the air. It was time to go. As he rose and walked through the wheat to the road, Donald felt slightly embarrassed by his own trepidation. He'd done any number of 'jobs' like this for the Lund brothers. He'd roughed up plenty of guys for far less. This was no different he told himself and loaded his hulking frame into the car. He turned the key and eased off the shoulder and back onto a road with no cause for correction in a landscape devoid of anomaly. With the shortest distance between two points being a line, here, just east of Williston, Donald possessed no excuse or other alternatives to keep him from his appointed round or from destiny, determined as much by time and temperament, as by a man's place within a specific geography. Donald's riches lay at the end of his fists which held the steering wheel tight now as the vehicle moved across land geologically rich beyond anything his reservation education would have allowed him to understand. The Manifest Destiny of Frank Lund and thousands of other white men just like him, some of whom had not even been born yet, lay patiently within Donald's curled, scar tissue tattooed knuckles. The land he had danced in reverence moments before was destined to be poked, prodded, and, by some folks' measure, desecrated; and unwittingly Donald Reddeer of the Mandan would have a hand in it. The ghosts of dead relatives he'd hoped to conjure were, by all accounts, just bones waiting to be drowned beneath dam-made lakes or dug up in the drilling and development that would come in the continued wake of progress, something his deceased ancestors knew much about.

CHAPTER TWENTY-EIGHT
North Dakota

*

"Around noon on April 4, 1951, Andrew (Blackie) Davidson, the drilling superintendent on a wildcat well east of Williston, set fire to a rag and flung it into the air. He watched as its trajectory met an invisible stream of natural gas that emanated from the ground, sending a flare thirty feet into the sky; by night fall, it could be seen ten miles away. There was oil in North Dakota."
- Eric Konigsberg (The New Yorker, 2011)

*

Domestic oil production was not an overriding concern in 1968, when the largest concentration in North America was discovered in Prudhoe Bay on the North Slope of Alaska. But things had changed over the following decades with the rise of OPEC, the oil crisis of 1973, and an almost consistent state of unrest in the Middle East. From 1970 to 2008, foreign oil dependence grew in the United States as energy consumption rose from fewer than fifteen million barrels a day to almost twenty million and domestic oil production fell from roughly eleven million barrels a day to about six million barrels. The cost at the pump for the consumer during the same period was excruciating, even when accounting for inflation, with prices going from an average of .40/gallon in 1973 to a disconcerting spike of $4.11/gallon in the summer of 2008. Over those forty years the lines between Democrats and Republicans were as discernible as those carving up the country into blue and red at election time with liberals calling for an increase in alternative energy sources and conservatives sounding the clarion call for more domestic drilling, even in the most politically polarizing environments including offshore, on federal lands, and in sensitive ecosystems such as the Arctic.

Just as the economy was collapsing in 2007, domestic oil producers found themselves in possession of the technology they needed to profitably drill for oil and natural gas in two of the largest fields in North America: the Williston Basin straddling the North Dakota/Montana border and the Marcellus Shale stretching from West Virginia through Pennsylvania up into central New York State. Just as the sleepy prairie town of Williston was being transformed by an influx of oil and gas companies eager to grab a share of these energy El Dorados, rural towns along the Appalachian chain in the east were being saved from the destitution of the economic collapse spurred by the home mortgage crisis gripping most of the rest of the country. These peripheral, nearly forgotten communities were not only saved, but given a national stature and status unimaginable by new software able to better model oil basins and horizontal drilling technology, both in conjunction with hydraulic fracturing or fracking as it has become ubiquitously known.

Geologist J.W. Nordquist of Phillips Petroleum verified the presence of oil in a three- hundred-and-sixty-million-year-old formation in the Williston Basin he named the Bakken after the family whose land it was discovered on. He described the formation as "an Oreo Cookie" due to the fact that of the formation's three-tier makeup. There lying between two layers of shale was a layer of dolomite which held the oil. The compact nature of the shale, though, made going after the play, as oil deposits are referred to, not viably profitable. The basin is now believed to hold twenty-five-thousand-square-miles of oil. Fracking, among other oil exploration technological advancements, had made it possible, at last, to extract this bounty from the Bakken Formation—very profitably.

CHAPTER TWENTY-NINE
Williston, North Dakota (2011)

"Wait in the truck."

Shannon lit a cigarette, blowing the smoke into Charlie's face.

"Anything you say, Charlie boy."

Charlie exited the truck and headed for the front door of his father's house. The day which had begun sun-kissed, but cold, had given way to gray clouds and light snowfall. At the door, Charlie hesitated, looked back to Shannon who gave him the finger, and turned back to knock only to find himself face to face not with his father, but with a strapping young man, a dead ringer for Charlie at the same age.

"Benjamin?"

"Who the fuck are you?" Then, after noticing Shannon sitting in the truck, Benjamin stepped onto the landing, his face just inches from Charlie's. "And what the fuck is she doing back here?"

"I'm…"

But before Charlie could finish speaking, Benjamin was backing him back down the sidewalk, shoving Charlie's shoulders as exclamation points to a tirade brought on by a sudden realization of whom Charlie was; a young lifetime's worth of anger spitting from Benjamin's lips.

"Now? Now you're here? Now? You rotten son of a bitch. Do you know what it was like growing up with her... that fucking junkie I have for a mother? Do you?"

Charlie didn't know, couldn't even begin to imagine. And now Benjamin was no longer shoving him, but punching him—in the face, in the chest, in the stomach—and Charlie didn't raise a hand to defend against the blows. And then he was on the ground, Benjamin kicking him in the ribs; the cursing from his son's lips like a bout of endless projectile vomiting. Charlie could hear Shannon screaming, but could not see that she was now out of the car, her arms wrapped around Benjamin's waist, trying to pull him back. Then a voice across the cold air could be heard as stinging as the shooting pain racing up and down Charlie's battered frame now curled into the fetal position.

"I said that's enough, Benjamin."

Charlie's right eye was already swollen shut, but through his left he could see his frail father, cane in hand, there on the landing.

"They can't hurt you anymore," Karl consoled Benjamin.

"Benjamin," slipped from Shannon's mouth in a cloud of condensation and Benjamin turned on a dime to face her, his fist at the ready.

Then there were sirens.

Shannon moved past Benjamin's coiled body, grabbed Charlie's hand and coaxed him to his feet, herding him into the car, then getting in the driver-side herself.

Benjamin moved to block them from leaving, but again Karl intervened.

"Let them go. They won't be back," adding cryptically under his breath, "I can guarantee it."

CHAPTER THIRTY
Williston, North Dakota (1947)

*

*"People sleep peaceably in their beds at night only because
rough men stand ready to do violence on their behalf."*
- George Orwell

*

All seemed quite. The windmill in the yard turned lazily. Clothes
on the clothesline waved as if saying hello—or goodbye. Donald
shut off the Packard and got out. He was unsteady, not from drink,
but from lack of it. He walked a crooked line to the farmhouse and
knocked hard on the screen door. He waited. He knocked again,
harder this time and when no one answered he let himself in. He
looked left—a living room. He looked right—a dining room which
led to the kitchen. He made his way that way, through the dining
room and into the kitchen where he began rifling cabinets until he
found his fix: a bottle of Old Fitzgerald, a sour mash bourbon, still at
half mast. He unscrewed the cap and took a long pull. Donald wiped
his brow. He often got the sweats with the shakes. He tipped the

bottle to his mouth a second time, but his lips were barely wet when he heard a voice.

"Turn around."

Donald shifted his large body, turning slowly until he was no farther than an arm's length from the barrel of a gun.

Standing there was Harlan, a shotgun raised and tucked deep into his shoulder.

"What the hell do you think you're doing?' Harlan demanded.

"I was thirsty. I'll leave. Don't shoot me, I'm just a drunk."

Harlan had always been sympathetic to the Native Americans around Williston and he understood their desperation when it came to stiff drink. There wasn't a package store in North Dakota that would sell to Indians.

"You can take the bottle, just get out of my house and don't come back or next time I'll shoot before I talk."

"I'm sorry."

Harlan lowered the shotgun. "Go ahead now, get out."

Donald was moved for a moment by the man's generosity, but only for a moment, after which he swung the bottle hard into the man's temple. And then they were both on the floor, the report of the shotgun which had gone off when it hit the floor ringing in Donald's ears. Stunned, but full of adrenaline, Donald rose to his feet not realizing he had been hit in the leg by the errant volley. The man lay on the floor, unconscious, bleeding from the head. Donald tried to think but couldn't. This was not the job. The job was to cripple the old man badly enough that it would make it impossible for him to work the acreage of his farm. Donald didn't know if he had killed him or not, but he did know committing a murder was a life sentence at best, a sure death sentence once they locked an Indian up with a bunch of white convicts for killing a white man. It was the Lund brothers who had put him up to this and Donald decided on the spot that it would be the Lund brothers who could figure a way out of this. And so with it settled within his mind, which could now only think of the case of beer awaiting him back in Mandan, Donald hoisted the man from the floor, throwing him over his back, and headed out of the farmhouse the way he had come in, confident he could get the dead weight he was carrying into the trunk of the Packard.

CHAPTER THIRTY-ONE
Stanton, North Dakota (1947)

Karl opened the trunk of the Delahaye, unstrapped the spare tire, and hoisted it out. Jacking up the car and removing the flat tire had taken better than an hour. The jack had kept sinking into the mud and now the driver-side rear of the car sat precariously tilted up after he had constructed a wobbly stone piling to give the whole rig enough purchase to do the job. In the meantime, Frank had wandered off with the two women back to the whorehouse and had yet to return. Karl knew there was no way he would make it back in time to see Marilyn and he thought of her, sitting there at home, looking out into the fading light of 10th Avenue, her heart rising then falling as cars approached then continued on down the tree-lined street. As he labored with the spare, trying as best he could not to knock the jury-rigged jack from beneath the car, he decided he would leave Frank's ass in Stanton as soon as the tire was secured. But then, as with every plan Karl had, it all evaporated with the sound of Frank's voice.

"Those two squaws could have changed that tire by now. Looks like you won't be getting in Hoff's daughter's pants tonight after all."

CHAPTER THIRTY-TWO
Williston, North Dakota (2011)

Charlie sat on a sunken gray couch which had surely once been white. He held an equally dirty washrag, knotted into a ball and filled with ice.

"You can fuck me if you want—I mean, if you're up to it."

Shannon walked from the kitchen area of her trailer to the area where Charlie was convalescing, which was really all the same area, and knelt down on the threadbare carpet beneath him. Her eyes were softer than they had been just hours before in the car. She might have just been coming down off of whatever she was usually on, but they were no longer wired, dilated, and full of contempt. They were blue. She had always had the most beautiful blue eyes. When they had first started dating in high school, it was those eyes that had sealed the deal for him. They were honest eyes; too honest at times, but he had always known where she stood by just looking into them. He knew where he stood now with her, but he didn't feel the same and he knew neither would she shortly. It was time for some honesty on his part. She took his hand and began to kiss it, taking a finger into her mouth here and there. He felt nothing, but it wasn't just for her. He pulled his hand away from her lips.

She looked off into a distance that wasn't there in the small trailer and spoke softly now, saying, "I know I'm not beautiful anymore."

"Yes you are."

She pushed herself from the floor and was standing now.

"You always were a liar, Charlie Lund," then adding, "You wanna see something fucked up."

He'd already seen enough fucked up shit since arriving back in Williston, but he nodded yes.

Shannon walked to the kitchen, to the sink, turned the water on and reached for a lighter near an ashtray on the counter. She held the lighter near the stream of water and flicked it with her thumb igniting it. The stream was a sudden lap of flame, but somehow still water. She turned to him.

"Pretty fucked up, huh?"

Turning back to the sink Shannon shut the tap off sending the smallest fizzle of smoke into the air which dissipated almost immediately. The room, which prior to the little chemistry experiment had smelled of bleach and mildew, now took on the odor of natural gas.

"You talked to anyone about this?"

"Just Bob Mosier over at the *Williston Herald*. Was probably the reason I got fired from the Lunch Box." Then defiantly, "Talkin' to him too much and standin' up to the trash from the oil fields pinchin' my ass and stiffin' me on tips."

"What did he say?"

Shannon began rooting around in a cabinet under the sink and answered distractedly, "Somethin' about methane and a bunch of other stuff that went right over my uneducated head."

"Well, he's right. There's methane in your well and not a surprise considering the amount of drilling going on around this casa. It's a direct effect of the fracking, you can bet on it."

Shannon turned on a heel triumphantly holding the bottle of vodka she kept stashed for when her blues got to be too much to deal with while sober.

"Wanna get drunk and fool around? You can tell me all about fracking while you're, well, you know."

Charlie noticed the slightest tinge of blush blossom across Shannon's cheek bones and the hard look she'd been sporting the past twenty-four hours left her face at last. She seemed to see something in him he could no longer see in himself. He knew she wanted to feel the same sense of hope and so against his own better judgment, his own true nature, he held out his hand. She, with her fading shadow in tow, moved from the kitchen to the couch, landing on his lap, the setting sun outside the trailer shooting its final tired rays through the broken blinds of the window behind them and across her bloodshot, blue eyes.

"Technically it's hydraulic fracturing, not fracking…" Charlie began.

*

*"(There's) never been one case – documented case – of
groundwater contamination
in the history of thousands and thousands of hydraulic fracturing
(wells)."*
- Senator James Inhofe, Republican/Oklahoma (April 2011)

*

Charlie was right. Fracking was a slang term for the process
which enabled companies like Cummins Energy to create fractures
in rock formations with limited porosity like the Bakken by injecting
fluid into cracks holding oil and natural gas to enlarge them; the
larger fissures allowing more oil and gas to flow out and into a
wellbore, where it could be extracted efficiently.

Three hundred and sixty million years after ancient marine life
began its fossilized march toward becoming the oil and gas deposits
held in the Bakken Formation, hydraulic fracturing offered the only
viable answer to how to cost effectively procure the USGS estimated
3.65 billion barrels of oil, 1.85 trillion cubic feet of
associated/dissolved natural gas, and 148 million barrels of natural
gas liquids lying on the U.S. side of this massive play; this one
stretching across northwestern North Dakota and northeastern
Montana and on up into Canada.

The oil fields of Saudi Arabia, as by way of example, exist as
easily accessible reservoirs where vertical drilling allows relatively
direct access to hydrocarbon reserves. The Bakken Formation on the
other hand—with its challenging porosity and permeability —had
always been resistant to the normally and naturally free flowing

outcomes of vertical drilling. Though the Bakken's rich reserves had been suspected since the late 1940's and confirmed in ever technologically advancing geological surveys in the decades afterward, its tightly packed, essentially trapped resource of oil and gas was both technically and economically beyond feasibility for extraction until the advent of hydraulic fracturing. Ironically, hydraulic fracturing had been around as long as the notion of oil in North Dakota. Although it was in Kansas and not North Dakota, the first hydraulic fracturing experiment was conducted in 1947 by the Stanolind Oil and Gas Company. True, it was unsuccessful, but its promise was enough to entice Halliburton Oil Well Cementing Company to patent and be granted exclusive license to the process in 1949.

The process, though, remained an expensive and unnecessary alternative given the prodigious and highly profitable reserves of cheap oil and natural gas available around the globe for most of the 20th century. But even as industrialized nations became drunk at a hydrocarbon party none could see ending any time soon, there were bellwethers pointing to the downside of the bell curve of peak oil production. Plays that seemed inexhaustible in Texas, Oklahoma, Azerbaijan, and Venezuela were exploited to extinction. Oil booms in towns such as McCamey, Texas and cities such as Baku, Azerbaijan became busts. What took millions of years of geological transformation to turn dead organic material beneath these areas into oceans of oil, took less than a handful of decades for governments and oil companies to tap dry of their non-renewable energy.

Facts are not anomalies and current global consumption of oil and gas foreshadows similar fates for even the largest, most easily accessible plays in the coming century. With current alternative energy sources slow in development, impractical in application, and too expensive to become ubiquitous even in the near future, the world's hydrocarbon-based economies have turned their attention to the once hard to reach, once unprofitable oil and gas deposits formerly held hostage in tar sands and between dense layers of shale, siltstone and sandstone; the latter an accurate geological snapshot of the Bakken Formation revealing the necessity for now cost-effective, but still highly controversial hydraulic fracturing to harvest its spoils. Hydraulic fracturing now allows access to the highly compacted and maddeningly scattered hydrocarbons in the Bakken Formation of the Williston Basin, but, some have asked, at what cost? With the EPA's, to date and at best, cavalier attitude toward the arguably highly toxic cocktail slurry of chemicals (including hydrochloric acid) which make up the highly pressurized water, regulation is nearly non-existent, exposing waterways and groundwater to contamination, the long term effects unknown for those who rely on wells, streams, and rivers within the localized areas such as those surrounding Shannon's trailer.

*

"The simple step of a courageous individual is not to take part in the lie."

\- Aleksandr Solzhenitsyn

*

The trailer was dark now. Shannon lifted her head from Charlie's shoulder and kissed his lips, but he did not kiss her back and so she pulled away.

Now his lips moved, uttering softly, "I don't want to. Not just with you, with any woman."

Shannon looked puzzled for the briefest of moments before the truth hung in the air between them, obvious and honest. She put a hand on his cheek.

"Is that why you ran away, Charlie?"

He nodded and then leaned forward resting his head against her breasts. She held him like a child, gently rocking back and forth, well aware—even in the pitch black of the room—that he was crying.

CHAPTER THIRTY-THREE
Stanton, North Dakota (1947)

Karl started the Delahaye, the tire changed at last. Frank, full of his usual bravado, in the backseat refused to let up.

"How come you never take a roll in the hay with the squaws up here? Are you queer or something?

They were headed out of Stanton on the usual unpaved road and Karl, staring blankly ahead, began to slowly accelerate. Karl's thoughts wandered as Frank laughed on at his expense.

In his mind's eye, Karl could see his foot continuing to push down on the gas pedal... causing the car to bump wildly... Frank's voice becoming panicked... Karl barely keeping control of the car as Frank shouts for him to stop... Karl steeling himself, gripping the steering wheel as tightly as possible before jamming on the brake... sending Frank hurdling over the front seat and into the windshield... his feet left dangling over the back seat... his neck broken and no longer really supporting his bleeding and battered head lying on the dash...

"Maybe that's why you were 4F. Everyone knows the army doesn't take pansies."

Frank's taunting and belittling continued unabated and Karl's fantasy of killing him dissolved as he guided the Delahaye cautiously into nightfall toward Bismarck, his murderous vision replaced by the thought of Marilyn waiting patiently, unaware of just how far Karl was away on a night they had planned to be closer than they ever had before.

CHAPTER THIRTY-FOUR
Mandan, North Dakota (1947)

Marilyn stood at the window, her eyes a tennis match of back and forth following cars as they approached then passed the house from either direction. Her father had one late night a month—poker at The Elks—and she had waited patiently over the past thirty days for this evening to arrive. And now she waited impatiently for Karl to arrive. Another car, not Karl's, made its way up the hill. It slowed as it approached the house. Even in the falling darkness she could see a man staring—seemingly, but impossibly—at her from inside the vehicle. Then it slid past the house, turned left at the intersection, and pulled to the curb. A young man got out of the car and started down the sidewalk. Marilyn squinted here eyes and they widened as she recognized the figure crossing the street that was now headed for the house. No sooner had *Christoph?* passed through her mind then he was there knocking at the door. A panic came over her and she muttered a quick prayer, hoping her Karl was okay, before opening the door.

"Christoph?"

Christoph raised a finger to his lips, shushing her, his eyes smiling, then whispering, "Here to pick ya' up? Take ya' to meet

Karl. Come on, he's waiting. Then he held out his hand, adding, "It's okay, he told me all about you two."

Though she despised Frank, she had always had a soft spot in heart for Christoph. He was younger than his twenty-one years, a kid still in so many ways. She trusted him. And so she took his hand, stepped out onto the landing, closing the door behind her, and walked up the hill, asking only before getting into his car, "Where are we going?'

Christoph opened the car door for her and with a wink offered reassuringly, "Karl wants it to be a surprise."

CHAPTER THIRTY-FIVE

Williston, North Dakota (2011)

Karl woke from a dream in the same chair where he sat, ate, and slept. He had not stepped foot in the bedroom he had once shared with Elsie since long before her death. The sitting room was dark and his mind drifted back almost sixty-five years. Beams from the headlights of the occasional car or truck passing by outside on Highway 1804 sliced through the room by way of the large windows turning the space into a macabre chamber of moving, menacing shadows. He had always hated the night. That was when most of Frank's biddings had played out over the six decades before and many of them were still fresh in his memory. He switched on a banker's lamp on the side table with a small yank of its chain. He looked at his wrinkled hands. He touched the lines' deep contours on his face. *The face of a monster*, he thought.

What had become of the good natured young man he had once been? Frank's sins had been his as well and he knew that now. He had always thought differently, that the animal instincts of his older brother were not his burden; that eventually he would walk away from it all, preserve the young man in love; not outrun his eldest sibling, but run away. And he had, but it had only been after it was too late and his own soul bore the tarnish of Frank's deeds and deals, damning Karl, in the process, to a life distant from the one of his dreams.

And now a reverie came over him so powerful he could see her face again as it had been when she smiled, when she laughed. He still thought of her, just as she was, especially in the summer of 1947 before everything went to hell in the autumn. It had been a forbidden love and that perhaps was what had made it so sweet and now so bittersweet. He closed his eyes, licked his chapped lips, and whispered her name into the room— "Marilyn."

He could still feel her lips on his; the last kiss, the first kiss, and all those in between they had shared. The passion of that final summer still sent a shiver across his sagging, veined, and liver-spotted skin; still sent a rush of warmth to his weathered face. She would have been his wife, should have been. His child would have had her pale glow, his fair curls, but instead his child was bronze with a shock of straight black hair. *Charlie, my bastard son,* he thought; a bastard only because he had never really been a father at all to him—poor, half-breed Charlie with his sad excuse for a father. A father who married out of guilt, who lived to work so as to keep the shame, shortcomings, and failures of his past at an ever increasing distance; a past that had kept pace just enough to finally catch him in the end.

He could no longer outrun the memories, regrets, and abject failings of that fall of '47. They haunted his nights now and all he had amassed here in Williston. His agricultural fortune, turned the oil fortune Frank had so presciently anticipated, was now but a frail stand of reeds between him and his restless thoughts of Mandan, Marilyn, and what might have been.

He turned out the light and sighed, wished silently not upon a star, but within his scarred heart that Shannon had killed him in her afternoon rage, made blood sport of what was left of the man sitting in this chair. In the dark, he sat alone with his fitful reminiscences a while longer before old age overruled young memories and he drifted off to sleep.

CHAPTER THIRTY-SIX

Somewhere between Williston and Mandan, North Dakota (1947)

"Get up. Come on, you, get up."

Donald could hear a voice, but was more aware of the pressure at the small of his back. He rolled over, groggy, the drool on his lips coated with gravel. Hovering above him in the darkness was the barely recognizable outline of a highway patrolman. The patrolman used his boot once more to prod Donald, this time the pressure was applied to his stomach.

"I said, get on your feet."

Donald sat up and the patrolman moved back a step, his hand at his gun-holstered hip, as Donald proceeded to crawl to a standing position.

"Turn around and face the car, hands flat on the roof."

As Donald complied he noticed the open gas cap of the Packard. Unable to cope sober all the way back to Mandan, he had pulled over for a few quick whiffs and apparently one too many.

"Whose vehicle is this, Chief?"

Chief? thought Donald, but didn't respond.

From the trunk of the Packard came a muffled voice, a thumping sound.

"What's in the trunk, Chief?"

"My wife."

The patrolman drew his gun and ordered Donald to open the trunk. Donald brought his arms back to his side and shuffled down the remaining length of the car until he was square in front of the trunk.

"Open it, Chief."

Chief, Chief, Chief.

Donald reached with his left hand, though he was right handed, and opened the trunk as ordered. There he was, Harlan, battered and bruised, but conscious. His eyes were as wild as the patrolman's who had not expected to see a white man in the trunk and in the stunned moment Donald wheeled around blindly with his right hand—now a large balled up fist—striking the officer so hard in the face that Donald could feel bone and cartilage collapsing. Before the patrolman could react he was on the ground, Donald's large shoe across the wrist of the hand that held the gun. Donald leaned in and then down with his full weight, a snapping sound beneath his heel acutely audible in the cold, autumn air. The other pronounced sound resounding in the crystalline atmosphere was that of Harlan's feet pounding down the pavement before abruptly turning to the swoosh and swish of a body on the run, arms flailing to make a path through the roadside wheat field, ripe for harvest.

Donald's mind was no longer foggy and he acted without hesitation, grabbing the gun and firing a round into the patrolman's head. Turning on a heel, Donald made his way to the car, slid behind the wheel, and started the engine. The wheels screeched as he turned the car one hundred and eighty degrees, pointing it and proceeding down the middle of the road in the direction Harlan had run off. Looking left then right again and again he spotted the bent wheat where Harlan had entered the field. Donald jerked the steering wheel and drove the car into the field, headlights illuminating Harlan's frenzied path, bumping along its circuitous route until at last Harlan appeared in the headlights. Donald pushed the accelerator then jammed on the brake, hitting Harlan and sending him into the air for a few feet and ultimately to the ground where he came to rest face down without further movement.

CHAPTER THIRTY-SEVEN

Somewhere between Stanton and Mandan, North Dakota (1947)

*

"It looked as if a night of dark intent was coming, and not only a night, an age."

\- Robert Frost

*

Karl drove the car in silence. Frank had been drinking heavily in the back and was in a chatty mood. It was now too late for Karl to make his date with Marilyn and Frank knew this. He knew other things as well.

"I could never leave Eleanor. I like to have my fun, but a decent man does what's right. I could have lived as a bachelor, no questions asked. Skinny fellas like you can't afford to. People end up thinking you like guys."

"What makes you think you're a decent man?" Karl questioned, breaking his silence.

"What makes you think I'm not, Karly boy?"

"For one thing the way you run the business; the way you throw your weight around town."

"And you don't, Karl?"

"I do what I'm told."

"Which is why you're not running the cement works. Pop knew who to hand it over to."

"He'd be proud of you. A bully proud of a bully," Karl offered by way of a backhanded compliment.

"See, you didn't serve, which is why you don't understand the way the world really works. You putzed around Mandan with your 4F while I was watching guys bleed to death, getting hands blown off, having legs sawed off to keep the gangrene from killing them. And that wasn't even the worst shit. You sat at the movies eating popcorn while you were watching those news reels about the Kraut death camps. I marched into one of them, saw the dead bodies piled up so high it didn't make sense; the smell so bad it could kill. And you know what it taught me? Huh, Karl?"

"War is hell?"

"That's how smart you are, Karl. You might have put a year in at ND State before you got homesick and quit, but you ain't too bright. What all that shit over there taught me was get them before they get you."

"Who?"

"Anybody who keeps you from living the way you want to, Karl. Anybody."

Those words rang in Karl's ears all the way back to Bismarck.

CHAPTER THIRTY-EIGHT
Mandan, North Dakota (1947)

Christoph was whistling as he drove along. Marilyn sat perfectly still, perfectly quiet, feeling a little uneasy with arrangement until Christoph turned onto the road she knew headed out to the cabin on the Missouri; a place she'd been with Karl many times over the summer.

"I know where we're going," she said, perking up.

Christoph broke from his tune, flashing a smile, then confirming. "Yup, but that ain't the surprise. You know old lover boy. He's a real romantic." Christoph reached beneath the seat and pulled a fifth of scotch into the space between them. He shook it as he asked, "Need a pop?"

"Oh, no thank you, Christoph."

Marilyn didn't drink. She knew women who did. Her mother had, which is why she didn't. Reality was challenging enough at times given her own tendency for occasionally feeling strange, mentally off balance. She wondered if that is what it felt like to be drunk.

"Come on, take a swig. Big night for the lovely couple, right?"

Marilyn was uneasy with this talk.

"It's just a date, Christoph, and I'd like to thank you for driving me."

"You wanna thank me?"

"Why yes, thank you, Christoph."

Christoph uncapped the pint and took along drink. Marilyn's unease returned and so she looked away from Christoph and out the window at the trees, now just shadows in the aftermath of nightfall, one after the other in endless animation on the side of the road. She began to count them as a way of coping, as a way to ignore her rapid heartbeat and growing anxiety pulsing uncomfortably between her chest and her head. She had to keep her mind from fraying as it sometimes did when she felt this way. *Twenty-one, two, three, four...forty-five, six, seven... sixty-six, seven, eight* and then they were there, pulling up to the cabin. *Thank god*, she thought.

Christoph parked, turned off the car, and sat staring straight ahead. He pulled at the pint again, licking his lips afterward.

"Where is Karl? The place is dark," Marilyn asked though afraid of the answer.

"Who?"

Christoph's demeanor changed and with it the expression on his face which was now frightening. And Marilyn was frightened, suddenly very frightened.

"Karl," Marilyn clarified though it did not need to be.

"I told you it was a surprise. What are you, stupid?"

Marilyn turned herself toward Christoph and, as emphatically as she could, demanded, "I want you to take me home. Now."

"He's down by the river. Come, he's waiting." And with that Christoph got out of the car and began walking around toward the passenger side. He paused at the front of the car and motioned to her with a wave of his hand, but Marilyn did not move, so he continued around toward her side.

Marilyn's anxiety was now full-fledged panic and without really thinking she fumbled as quickly as she could through the interior of the car locking each door and ending up in the well of the backseat, crouching her knees and elbows tucked into the floorboards.

In a sing-song voice Christoph began to bait her as he circled the car again and again pulling at the door handles. "Mari-lyn, come out, come out wherever you are."

And then it was quiet. It was quiet for a long time save for Marilyn's hyperventilating. She had to think, but her mind had become a series of threads and each thought she had about what she should do only frayed further her fragile mental state. Then he was there again. His voice had dropped an octave it seemed as he began to intone slowly, "Little pig, little pig, let me in or I'll huff... and I'll puff... and I'll," before stopping short and the sound of breaking glass filled the car along with a rush of cool night air perfumed with river water and fallen leaves.

The fury of the initial moments inside the vehicle which immediately followed the shattering of the window was indescribable, but was only the opening salvo of the hell she would have to endure over the next thirty minutes.

CHAPTER THIRTY-NINE
Williston, North Dakota (2011)

Karl awoke abruptly for the second time since falling asleep in his chair. Somebody was in the room. He sensed it. He had always been a light sleeper and the nocturnal impediment had only worsened over the decades.

He called out in a low, phlegm-filled voice, asking, "Who's there?"

But there was no answer. The house was quiet, but outside the low rumble of distant water truck traffic persisted as it always did. The clock ticked on the mantle and as he became more lucid, less groggy, he became aware of it and looked to see that it was just after 1:00 a.m. Beyond the room's windows, darkness was still resisting dawn and his restless night had made him edgy and irritable, erasing the depression which had enveloped him a few hours before. He was again his old, cantankerous self. Irritated, he pushed his hands against the arms of the overstuffed chair, attempting to stand, but failing at first, wanting to rise and have a look around. The ghost of Frank had never stopped haunting his psyche and he mused for a moment that his brother's specter was in the room. He shuddered at the thought, a wave of goosebumps rippling down both arms. There was a presence in the room and it was evil.

CHAPTER FORTY

Somewhere between Mandan and Williston, North Dakota (1947)

The headlights of the Packard split the night in two, sliced through distance but seemingly not time. For Donald, time seemed to have stopped, to have even backtracked after what had transpired on that roadside just a few miles and minutes before. A cop was dead, the man from the farm too. Donald tried not to think of either. His skin was crawling. He hadn't had a real drink since the night before. The patch of illuminated pavement beyond the windshield began to move in waves. He was of this earth, but somehow not and shook his head back and forth in an attempt to sober up to the reality of his situation though he was as far away from drunk than he normally allowed himself to get. Then he heard a voice.

Donald looked to his right half expecting to see the dead patrolman seated next to him. But sitting there was a man he had only ever heard about through stories told by elders at the reservation while he was growing up: Mah-tó-he-hah. The Mandan medicine man the white man called Old Bear had been dead for at least one hundred and fifty years, but there he was in the flesh. He spoke again.

"Mihapmak."

It was a greeting from the Mandan language, a language Donald had grown up hearing but not speaking, though he understood it. It was a friendly greeting, but nothing about Mah-tó-he-hah seemed friendly. Donald thought of the vulture which had menaced him earlier that day. Now a long dead Mandan medicine man was talking to him. Donald wondered if he himself was already dead and the thought alone provided such a sense of relief that he began to hear in earnest what Old Bear was saying. Donald effortlessly translated in his head the Mandan language being spoken, but his momentary serenity faded the more Mah-tó-he-hah spoke.

"A man may walk away, even run away from himself, but the sun knows his deeds, the moon knows his deeds for they both know a man's shadow and a man only leaves his shadow behind in death. Your deeds have cheated a man not only of his shadow, but of his unborn child which will never be born now that it cannot be conceived. It is upon you to care for this nameless, faceless child whose spirit you alone have condemned to the darkness. Take this child."

Donald who had been looking away, listening while staring through the windshield into the dim headlights' rolling glow amidst the abyss of opaque prairie beyond, behind and beside him, now looked to Mah-tó-he-hah who held a small, lifeless baby, so pale it appeared almost light blue, lying limply in his palms. As Mah-tó-he-hah began to sing an old Mandan lullaby, blood appeared upon his lips, smearing around his mouth as he sang, dripping onto the dead child as the sound of his voice became more like the wail of a wounded animal, the words lost in a babble of high-pitched squeals and sanguineous gurgling.

But the car was empty, save for Donald and the one passenger in the trunk that had been with him since Williston. And so he drove on, tears blurring his vision, rolling down his cheeks; the taste of their salt swallowed in sob after shuddering sob.

CHAPTER FORTY-ONE
Mandan, North Dakota (1947)

Terror-stricken, Marilyn whimpered and cried out loudly, alternating back and forth between feelings of humiliation and rage as Christoph slammed in and out of her. She felt nauseous; sickened by him, and oddly, by herself. The pain between her legs was excruciating, but the pain in her heart was far worse. How could she have been so stupid, so naïve, so gullible? His breathing was like a train, like the trains in the Mandan railyard that came to a stop in steaming hot hisses and in metallic groans which she could hear late at night while she lay in bed awake but dreaming of the new day dawn would bring. This night would not end she thought; no new dawns would come even if the sun rose upon her tomorrow and every day after her Maker had marked upon her soul before sending her into this world. She tried to think of something, anything besides this vicious, degrading carnal act; this animal fate. She focused on her mother.

Marilyn forced her mind to flee the terror, fear, pain, and panic which held it captive and pictured herself floating away from her own body, until she hovered above the violence of Christoph's rape of her; above but not beyond its barbaric and vile grunting and heaving below in the backseat of the car.

Somehow, somewhere in the midst of this disgusting and insufferable battering and brutalizing hell she found the little girl again in the garden, picking peas as her mother fussed over her large vegetable garden. Her mother's favorite dress had been white and patterned in blue polka dots. Marilyn could see her in it, watering, weeding, wiping at her brow. Her mother was truly given to whimsy when Marilyn was little and she thought of how safe she felt then as her mother flitted between one whim and the next; painting bedroom walls in peculiar colors, putting on plays for Marilyn, practicing bird calls for hours seated on a stool in the yard where she had hung a dozen different feeders, holding broken bits of saltines in her palm and waiting patiently for small songbirds to alight. She often brushed Marilyn's hair for an hour straight while telling fantastical stories of make-believe kingdoms with flying woman and talking animals. Her hair had always been important to her and a source of pride; a gorgeous and striking red she claimed to have gotten from her own Irish grandmother which she styled differently almost daily based on photos of movie stars from popular Hollywood gossip magazines which she procured in Minneapolis on father's business trips they tagged along on. She often said that she herself was not beautiful, but that God had given her hair like fire to spark men's hearts instead.

Marilyn thought of her own hair which was ordinary by comparison, but which she too took great pride in each day, styling and brushing, fussing with it each morning until she was pleased with what she saw in her dressing mirror. It had been no different today, especially in anticipation of seeing Karl. She had chosen her most prized hair combs, which had been her mother's most prized as well; a pair which were gilded, stamped metal, Victorian-era and fashioned to look like butterflies. And now they were pinching, stabbing at her with each disgusting thrust from Christoph pushing her head back and forth into the car's backseat. And with this feeling, this thought, she floated back down into her tortured, now alien to her, body, and reached a hand to the side of her head, running her fingers over the form of the butterfly, feeling its wings, its ridges, and filigree. She was safe once again as she pictured them in her mother's hair.

He was finishing now and he thrust twice more before letting his body go limp, the full weight of him upon her now, a guttural but deflating moan leaving his lips. She unhinged the comb between her fingers, grasping the delicate butterfly form and pulling it with its two long, metal prongs from her hair. Tightening her arm, her wrist, and her hand, she thrust the hair comb toward Christoph's face twice in quick succession as forcefully as she could in the small available arc between their faces; the second time stabbing him so hard that her hand returned without the comb which was now protruding from Christoph's right eye.

And then she was running away from the car and through the overgrowth of the rutted drive, across the road which led to the cabin, and into the woods beyond. And she kept running, pausing only briefly once as a car roared past her, beyond her tree-obstructed view, out on the road, heading back toward town where she was headed herself toward a future much changed from what she had imagined when the day had begun.

CHAPTER FORTY-TWO

Bismarck, North Dakota (1947)

Karl pulled the Delahaye to the curb in front of the Elks and parked. It was late now and all his plans were up in flame, frustratingly entangled with the smoke from the cigar Frank was puffing on in the back of the car.

"Let me buy you a drink, Karl. It's the least I can do since that flat tire cost you your date with Carolyn."

"Marilyn. Her name is Marilyn."

"Oh, yeah, right. Well, you might as well drown your tears in some bourbon and if we're lucky, the poker game is still going on. You can at least take some of old man Hoff's money, if you can't take his daughter's virginity."

The last thing Karl wanted to do was spend another minute in Frank's presence, but he thought he'd at least stick his head in the door of the club to see if Hoff was still there for the regular, once-monthly poker night that almost no Elk ever missed. If he were lucky, he'd be there and Karl could at least head in the direction of Marilyn's, apology in tow, knowing John Paul was still otherwise occupied.

"Let's get that bourbon then," Karl demanded, before exiting the car and heading for the door.

Frank poured himself out of the vehicle and onto the sidewalk, proceeding a bit unsteadily toward the door himself, the liquor he had downed since leaving Stanton perhaps making rubber bands of his legs, but not fogging his mind in the least. Scores were to be settled, a future secured, and barriers to the bigger picture dismantled. They were already in motion and he simultaneously thought of the jobs Christoph and that big, dumb Indian should have concluded by now. It was time to celebrate, even if it was a bit premature of him to do so.

Frank entered the Elks behind Karl and took in the room in one sweep of eyes from the bar to the back room and the tables in between filled with Elks betting, anteing, drinking, smoking, laughing, and bantering. This was Frank's kingdom, a ready made audience half in the bag and throwing money around like kids pitching their pennies against curbs in town. Motioning to the barkeep with a twist of his finger in the air and as Karl stood flat-footed perusing the room, Frank headed toward the tables, the waitress, just moments later, delivering his double bourbon as he patted Elks on the shoulders, shook hands and made the usual spectacle of himself.

Karl scanned the lodge a second time, but Hoff was nowhere to be seen. His shoulders slumped in final defeat. Frank had won again and the sight of him cajoling with the assembled Elks filled him with a hollow, ineffectual rage. It was then and there, standing in the smoke and boozy atmosphere of the lodge, that he made a sober and clearheaded decision. He would no longer do Frank's bidding, no longer be at his beck and call, and no longer wait to make a life for himself with the woman he loved. Tomorrow morning he would finish with Frank's business, would meet Donald, pay him the bounty he had earned, and would drive away from the cabin and all of its ambiguous tortured and happy memories, the engagement ring which had been burning a hole in his pocket all week in hand, and head for Hoff's house where he would get down on one knee on the doorstep if he had to, and ask for Marilyn's hand. He didn't need a drink anymore, he needed some air to let his thoughts of, prayers for a new day free to wander the cold night's stars in hopes they would rise to meet the new day with the same conviction of the sun. He turned to walk out and his breath left his body at the sight of Christoph coming through the door, a hand across an eye, his face blood-crusted and fixed with pain.

Christoph dropped his hand from his face and grabbed Karl by the lapels of his suit coat, shouting above the din, "Where the fuck is Frank?"

His right eye, if one could still call it that, was a mass of black blood and swelling, the lid over it seemingly stitched in place by the clotted pool covering it, the blonde eyebrow above it devoid of its fair brush of color.

The "What the hell happened to you?" from Karl's mouth boomed and bounced around the now quiet room, table after table of Elks staring in their direction. Frank made a beeline toward his brothers as an ironic, distant whistle blow of a locomotive coming into Mandan across the river made for the perfect metaphor for the head of steam with which he approached. But Karl no longer cared and he shoved Christoph away forcefully and walked out the door into a future glimpsed, but still uncertain.

BOOK 2

Secrets, Innuendos, and Deceptions

CHAPTER FORTY-THREE

Mandan, North Dakota (1947)

*

"But the beauty is in the walking. We are betrayed by destinations."

- Gwyn Thomas

*

The street lights of Main Street in Mandan were macabre, casting Marilyn's shaking, frail shadow to the pitted sidewalk as she walked holding the tatters of her dress as close across her breasts as the now forlorn frock would allow. She caught a glimpse of herself in a shop window and stood a moment to stare at her violated image. She had aged ten years and she could see for the first time the bite mark on her cheek. Looking more closely, she could see the individual teeth marks indenting her skin. She felt their marks upon her very soul along with her own humiliation and shame.

Lost in this embittered and barely recognizable reflection, Marilyn had not at first noticed the police car that had pulled along the curb behind her, but now the mirror image of her face was surrounded by a blinking carousel of red light coming from atop the vehicle behind her. She turned to see Officer Walt Schefter approaching her. She held out a hand in an attempt to halt his progress, to keep him from seeing up close what she had seen in the store window, but it was too late, he had seen her disheveled, torn and frayed visage clearly enough as he had approached her on his patrol down Main Street that he had been compelled to pull over; especially given the hour and what appeared to be a half clad woman staring blankly into the hardware store's large plate glass display area where mannequins with rakes in their hands stood mime over a scatter of real fallen leaves that had been swept from the street and placed beneath their immobile feet.

"Marilyn?" Officer Schefter queried, his recognition of her at once certain, but riddled with disbelief.

"I'm fine. I'm just headed home."

Officer Schefter, in front of her now, stepped back a single step and looked her up and down, only glancing at, but quickly noting her savagely torn dress and her barely covered bosom, before his gaze landed on her bruised and bitten cheek.

"What on earth happened to you?"

He slipped out of his own police jacket and moved to drape it across her shoulders but she hissed at him, sounding just like a feral alley cat.

"Don't you dare touch me."

He reached again with the jacket, begging, "Please, let me take you to the hospital."

With those words Marilyn's mind finally gave way and she became unglued. The hospital is where they had first taken her mother when they had found her in a more advanced state of undress a year before. Her mother never came home and Marilyn feared a similar fate was about to befall her.

Marilyn swept her hands, fingers curled, nails jutting, at the jacket and clawed it to the ground. She began to not just scream, but screech at Office Schefter, accusing, "This is what you did to my mother. This is what you did. What you did! What you did! What you did!" Then turning to the plate glass display window she flung herself arms first into it, shattering it and ending up with half her body on either side of the pointed remnants, her feet still on the sidewalk, back bent with her stomach hovering precariously above the jagged horizon of remaining glass, her bloody palms flat against the tawny, dried leaves beneath the father/son mannequin pair whose dead, painted eyes now appeared stunned and shocked instead of wistfully glinted by their autumnal preoccupation.

*

Karl walked the deserted stretch of road toward the cabin. Trees on either side, nearly leafless, towered overhead, their bare limbs ominous and menacingly animated in the wind blowing down from the north. Winter would not be waiting long before arriving. He could remember as a child trick-or-treating through snowdrifts to make his Halloween rounds for the popcorn balls and nuts most neighbors doled out. He had been a happy-go-lucky kid who possessed neither the confidence nor good looks of the older brother he worshipped. Frank had yanked his chain and pulled his strings even then; baited and berated him into any number of delinquent teenage acts from shoplifting to random incidents of property damage. These behaviors had been contrary to his actual nature, which was to be kind and caring. But he had done so as a way of gaining favor with Frank, favor which was at best fickle or altogether unavailable.

Ironically, Frank had always been especially protective of Christoph who had never really needed his protection. Nevertheless, Frank's favor often fell upon his baby brother, while Karl was made to jump through hoop after flaming hoop to prove his loyalty and his mettle. Within the rhythm of his footsteps and the whistling melody of the wind, Karl's thoughts danced backward through time as he walked on toward the final movement of a symphony he and his brothers had constructed, but which Frank had always conducted. He wasn't sure at what point he had begun to think for himself, but it was clear he had turned a corner when he left Christoph and his blind eye behind at the Elks. He now turned the corner where the road met the grassy, leaf-strewn drive up to the cabin and the raw and unpredictable Missouri River of his childhood, its mud still pulsing through his veins and mixed with his blood— a Missouri River about to be tamed by uncountable yards of concrete for the good of all and by the greed of Karl's older brother. Leave it to Frank to have a hand in changing the course of a mighty waterway and to Karl to be still paddling like hell to get out of an eddy. Dawn was breaking on a man who hadn't slept and over a river moving tiredly as it often did in the fall. A past was about to be put to rest.

CHAPTER FORTY-FOUR

Williston, North Dakota (2011)

Charlie jerked awake to the distinct ring and tingling vibration of a text coming in on his phone. He pulled it from a pocket of his jeans which he had slept in on Shannon's couch. Shannon's bedroom door was open and he could see the bed was unmade but she was not in it. An uneasy feeling came over him. She was a junkie and he knew junkies could only go so long before they needed a fix. He cracked the blind behind the couch and noted it was well past dawn by the bright light casting a cheery aura over the desolate landscape outside the trailer. Shannon's Torino was gone.

He checked the text which informed him he was to report to work, despite the fact that he'd been given two weeks off for the melee in the parking lot just the day before. He welcomed it, although he was leery of a ten hour day in the water truck with nothing but his thoughts to keep him company. He knew he'd made a mistake the night before confiding in Shannon after twenty years that he liked men, not women. God only knew what a well-methed or needle-loosened tongue would say or to whom. With that thought he panicked, stood, and pawed at his back pockets. Of course, his wallet was gone.

*

Shannon pounded on the door of Room 119, trying to rouse Dawes in hope of continuing her meth high. She'd spent every bill that had been in Charlie's wallet getting high with a trucker parked for the night at the Pilot truck stop out on Highway 2. Shannon knew she could always find the crank she needed at the truck stops which had popped up all over Williston since the oil and gas boom began a few years earlier. Problem was she usually didn't have the money which never stopped her from heading out to Pilot, the Flying J, Ironwood, or, the unfortunately named, Love's. Somebody was always willing to part with a little crystal meth for a hand job, a blowjob, or a fuck which never lasted long despite the amount of amphetamine, coke, meth, and 5 Hour Energy sluicing its way around most truckers' veins. Heterosexual, homosexual, and bisexual encounters of every sort and sordid description could be found going down. She made a mental note to tell Charlie about these various hotspots in case he needed to snuggle with some good old boy in the back of a rig's cab. She'd been in plenty of them, but now she wanted a bed to stretch out on and a free fix or six from Dawes.

The door opened, Dawes squinting. He was fully dressed, from work boots to belt to the sweat bandana he often had tied across his forehead.

"What fuckin' time is it?"

"I don't fuckin' know, Dawes. Let me in, I need a taste."

Dawes, though barely awake, grabbed his crotch. "I bet you do."

"Pervert."

"There's some blow on top of the TV. I'm going back to sleep. I been out all night."

"Over at the Flying J giving long haulers hand jobs," Shannon jibed with a giggle.

"You know I hate to hear you talk about yourself that way… although, I could use a hand job come to think of it."

Shannon pushed past Dawes and headed for the TV. Dawes closed the door on the too bright world beyond his motel man-cave. He could be late for work and he knew it.

CHAPTER FORTY-FIVE

Mandan, North Dakota (1947)

"I want my money and the beer."

"I have your money, but what the hell happened to my car?"

Karl, who had been sitting on the cabin porch since arriving, walked under a bright morning sun and around the front of his new Packard, which was covered in mud and had what looked like wheat sticking out of the gap between the bumper and the frame.

"I had a problem."

Frank's Delahaye appeared at the bottom of the drive and slowly made its way up the ruts until it came to a stop near Karl's Packard. Frank got out of the back and Christoph, holding a bar towel from the Elks over his eye, got out from behind the wheel.

"What happened to that new Packard of yours, Karl?" Frank asked not really caring.

"Let's get this over with, Frank," Karl answered.

Christoph lowered the towel from his face and Donald grimaced at the gruesome eye socket he found himself staring into. "What happened to you?"

Christoph stepped toward Donald menacingly and threatened, "None of your fucking business, Tonto."

"That's right. None of this is my business. I just want my money and a ride back to town. But not in this car."

Donald gestured toward the Packard.

"A ride wasn't part of the deal, Donald," Frank informed him and then asked, "Did you fix that guy in Williston or not?"

Donald walked around to the trunk of the Packard and opened it. The Lund brothers followed and saw for themselves Harlan's broken and lifeless body.

Karl, aghast, blurted out, "Jesus Christ, Donald. You killed the fuckin' guy?"

"Son of bitch had a shotgun. I got buckshot in my leg."

Frank leaned in and looked at Harlan whose eyes were fixed and frightened as though he'd seen a ghost.

"There's a dead cop too somewhere between here and Williston. He shouldn't of asked me to open the trunk."

Frank turned to face Donald and pulled a handgun from where it had been tucked into his waistline. He pointed it at Donald's head and asked a question which begged no answer. "Are you out of your fucking mind?"

"Shoot the big dumb fuck, Frank," Christoph implored.

"Hold on, hold on," Karl pleaded.

"Shut the fuck up, Christoph. Don't ever tell me what to do. Karl's going to shoot him. He's the one who screwed up this job. Although I ought to shoot you, Christoph. How fucking stupid are you, you fucking one-eyed jack?"

Frank started to hand the gun to Karl whose hands remained at his side, but abruptly turned and struck Donald in the face with it, dropping him to his knees, where Frank proceeded to pistol whip him while Donald tried in vain at once to rise to his feet and to cover his face with his large hands. Frank beat him until Donald's eyes finally rolled back in his head and he hit the ground.

"I ain't stupid, Frank. I did what you told me to," Christoph answered as if it were not a rhetorical question Frank had asked.

"Shut the fuck up, Christoph. I never told you to do nothing but scare her off. You never could keep your dick in your pants. It's not enough I gotta clean up Karl's messes, now I gotta clean up yours? Maybe Karl oughta shoot you too."

"What in God's name are we talking about here?" Karl shouted, "Nobody's gonna shoot anybody."

Karl grabbed the gun from Frank who did not resist letting it be taken from him.

"You wanna tell him, Christoph, or should I?

"Tell me what?" Karl demanded.

"Lover boy fucked your girlfriend last night, but by the looks of things it got a little rough in the backseat. Isn't that what you told me at the Elks, Christoph?

Karl was dumbstruck for a moment, but quickly it began to dawn on him that this wasn't just one of Frank's cruel jokes. His brain was a mass of overloading wires. His hand shook as he raised the gun and pointed it at Christoph. He shouted, spittle flying from his lips, "Tell me it isn't true, Christoph! Tell me, say it you little bastard!"

But Christoph, did not speak. He raised the towel to his eye, dabbing at it.

The yard began to spin and Karl blinked hard in an effort to try to stop it, but the rage pulsing through his body opened his eyes wide and there amidst the revolving carousel of trees and brush was Christoph smirking. Karl clenched his teeth and, as a vein appeared blue and raised upon his neck, turned the gun away from Christoph and placed it against his own temple. A bullet would be the salve to his torment.

Then he hit the ground, hard. His head throbbing from the impact, his eyes blurry and staring at the wide Dakota sky beyond Frank's frame which straddled him, the gun now in his older brother's hand, pointed directly at his forehead.

"Don't say I never did anything for you."

Karl squinted his eyes hard to close them tight.

Bam!

The sound of the gunshot echoed down the river and faded as quickly as it had come.

Christoph grabbed his chest and fell to his knees. He tried to speak, but blood poured from his mouth. He sputtered, viscous red liquid spitting from his lips, then collapsed on the gravel. And there he lay, dead.

Frank rolled off Karl and got to his feet. The weight of his brother gone now, Karl sat straight up, hyperventilating as he blurted out in fits and starts, "What... the fuck's... wrong... with you? My God... Frank."

And then he pushed himself from the ground and lunged at Frank who stopped him dead in his tracks, pointing the gun at him.

"Uh, uh, don't be stupid. You're up to your ass in trouble and the only shot you have at making things right is to listen very closely, brother. First things first."

Frank turned, pointed the gun at Donald who lay unconscious just feet away from Christoph's lifeless body and fired a bullet into Donald's brain. Donald moved just slightly, but didn't make a sound.

Karl, his mind a whirl of panic, fear, and no longer fight, but flight began running down the gravel drive.

A bullet whizzed past his head and he stopped and turned around.

"You're in deep shit, Karl. You hired this fucking totem pole. He was supposed to beat that guy in Williston so he'd have to spend the rest of his life in a wheelchair, not until he was dead. He's in the trunk of your car, not mine. So, get your ass back here if you don't want to live the rest of your days in a prison cell. Big brother's gonna fix this and you're gonna help."

Karl knew he was right. He stuck his hand into his pocket and rolled the ring box around in his hands. There was no chance of anything if he didn't help Frank. Once again, Frank had played him.

"Christoph's a suicide, get it? And Donald and this body in your trunk are going to disappear. Give·me a hand."

Karl was numb, but began walking back toward the cars, well aware that to fix this, to have a chance at happiness he would have to respond not react. *But what of Marilyn? Was she suffering even as he stood here? Would she even see him?* Karl's mind was a tangle of unanswered, unanswerable questions, but to find out the answers he would be forced to cast his fate with his older brother. Karl was suddenly lucid and announced much to Frank's surprise, "Let's do this."

But his lucidity was extremely compartmentalized. What Karl should have accepted by now given the events of the past twenty-four hours, but couldn't allow himself to, was that although he was still among the living amidst the carnage, he was probably already dead to Marilyn.

CHAPTER FORTY-SIX
Williston, North Dakota (2011)

Karl could see his killer as he floated above his body seated limply in the chair below in the wake of his murder. He had never seen it coming, but had given no resistance once it began. He was above the house now, a beautiful dawn breaking in the east throwing sharp pink and muted orange into a cyclorama of a sky the bluish hue of veins beneath skin. Karl could see the extent of the significant acreage he had called home for six decades and his seemed to be the only without an oil derrick sticking out of it. Worldly thoughts gave way as Williston disappeared beneath the clouds and now it was his spirit which spoke to him in a whisper repeating only her name; *Marilyn, Marilyn, Marilyn, Marilyn, Marilyn,* until she was there and without a word all was understood between them that was once misunderstood, at once forgiven then forgotten. She became only light as he became only light and his last thought before drifting away into a peace he had never known was that his penance had been to live.

CHAPTER FORTY-SEVEN
Williston, North Dakota (2011)

Rain cried its way down the windshield of the water truck. Charlie had been driving back and forth to the same frack site all morning. The sky was steel wool above the prairie and begged for reverie the way a blue wash and bright sun cannot. He had given himself to it the past few hours; settled into the melancholy he was prone to, slouched deep into the driver's seat; a puddle of a man splashing sullen memories into the warm cab air which hung suspended for a moment before being swept aside by the rhythm of the wipers. The taste of ozone moved from nostrils to tongue with each breath. He had almost all but forgotten the silken quality of light spring rainstorms brought to the North Dakota sky; comforting and unsettling in the same swallow; the teary-eyed, blinking relief of exhalation immediately followed by the ominous, furrowed brow foreshadowing of inhalation, both so electric he could feel the hair on his arms at attention and quivering above his skin. Something bad was going to happen or had already happened; he was sure of it.

It had been a rainy day in the Keys a year before when a similar premonition had come over him while finishing the last day of a spotty month's worth of work doing an on again, off again rehab job for a local restaurateur who hired him sporadically out of pity after the housing bubble took its toll on the construction work in Florida; but also because they had been lovers a decade before and had remained friends after that bubble burst. Michael, whom he had met and become involved with in the aftermath of this failed relationship, was to have met him in the restaurant bar after work, but he never arrived. Charlie found him at home hanging from a beam in the garage. It became a minor scandal in the condo association where they had cohabitated, sharing a sometimes complicated but mostly conventional life together. Despite beliefs to the contrary, it wasn't any easier to be gay in the Sunshine State than say in Nebraska. And also contrary to the talk around the condo complex in the aftermath of Michael's death, homosexuals commit suicide for the same reasons heterosexuals do, but unlike them, face the prejudicial reality that when a gay man uses a belt to hang himself whispers of autoerotic asphyxiation are as inevitable as they are absurd. Michael had been no more, no less complicated than someone like Shannon. Charlie had had sex with women, sex with men and his own demons had been consistent and persistent in either gender's bed. At twenty-five, though, he had had enough of what his longtime shrink called fake adulthood; the one spent emulating one's father, one's mother, mimicking their lives, their supposed path to happiness. It had been twenty years since he had slipped away into the vastness of a country content to hide him from a marriage and impending fatherhood—the dual, default leitmotifs of his peer group at the time in Williston.

As Charlie fell deeper beneath the hypnotic cadence of the wipers, his thoughts turned to his mother, the beautiful and gentle

Elsie. It had always been she, much to Karl's consternation, who had indulged Charlie's sensitive side with art, music lessons, and almost limitless trips to the library where they both would wade the few stacks for hours browsing, reading, re-shelving, and repeating this triptych ad nauseum. She neither promoted nor discouraged dating, but was at the ready with homemade corsages and boutonnières for the dances Charlie did attend with this classmate or that classmate on his arm; female classmates all of them of course, especially in 1980's North Dakota—an era and a place where the few suspected gay students were bullied and bruised emotionally and physically into submission. The truth was it hadn't gotten all that much better in the thirty subsequent years.

It had also been Elsie who had encouraged Charlie to go to college instead of staying on to help manage the family's substantial farming acreage. But there had never been a question in his young mind and so with Elsie's blessing and Karl's expectations he had shipped off to North Dakota State under the false pretenses that he was to study Ag-Chem to keep his father happy to pay the bill. It was there that his appetite for literature and the arts blossomed into full-fledged gluttony. There the stacks held more than dry tomes on soil evaluation and erosion studies, and much more in terms of classics than the little public library in Williston. This particular candy store was full of literary sweets the likes of Tolstoy, Turgenev, Pushkin, and Gogol and he had soon begun to miss classes and then fail classes while holed up in the library. But it was there, before his father finally did stop paying the bill, that he had tasted something else sweet for the first time: another young man's lips.

But upon returning to Williston he had fallen back in with the old crowd, one of whom had been Shannon. Technically, Charlie had initially been bisexual, a fact he kept well-hidden from the toughs and tramps of Williston, and eventually he caved to both Shannon's stoned-out come-ons and his father's sober demands by becoming a married man and a farmer with little thought of gay liaisons or the wider world beyond his prairie purgatory where he spent the next few years further disappointing his father and growing apart from a wife with whom he was only really playing house until she announced she was pregnant. And then he had run, run to the far corners of the Lower Forty-Eight and into the beds of as many men who would have him; into a life his father could never have guessed at, would never have accepted. But this was why he had returned; to tell Karl at last who his son really was, before it was too late.

The two-way radio in the cab crackled to life startling Charlie and putting an end to his poor man's version of À la recherche du temps perdu. It was Wendell Krouthammer back in the personnel trailer and he spoke emphatically through the static. "Charlie, you better bring it in, there's a police officer who needs to talk with you."

CHAPTER FORTY-EIGHT

Mandan, North Dakota (1947)

The advantage of the small, rural, still backwater town of Mandan was its basically gullible, backwater police department. Frank and Karl had simply strategized for a few minutes after casting their fates together, cleaned up and propped the area, practiced their rehearsed theatrics, and called in that they had found Christoph's body. The hardest part, besides loading Donald Reddeer's body into the trunk of Frank's car, was seeing Christoph. Karl had had a hard time keeping himself composed as they moved about the body, deciding where the gun would have fallen if in fact Christoph had shot himself. At one point Karl announced he couldn't go through with it. Despite their decided and coordinated, workmanlike efforts, it was in fact his little brother lying there. Frank, who usually met such weakness of character with derision and pointed brickbat, was uncharacteristically sensitive and told a rather lengthy story about the kind of guys in his platoon that made it out alive and the ones who didn't. He ended by saying he had known after returning from overseas that Christoph wouldn't make it, said Christoph had a funny little look in his eyes same as his dead buddies. As macabre as the scene was, Karl and Frank found themselves swapping fond or funny anecdotes about their little brother as they waited to perform their charade and before they knew it a few squad cars and an ambulance were pulling up the drive.

The fact was that most of the Mandan P.D. were on the take from Frank, including the four cops who showed up to "secure" the scene and interview Karl and Frank. Frank had just gotten done spinning a yarn about Karl firing Christoph the day before for making a crude comment about Marilyn Hoff, Karl's soon to be fiancé. They figured Christoph had exacted his revenge on her as a way of "getting back at him" as he put it to the nodding cops; finishing his just-connect-the-dots performance while he and his captive audience leaned across the back of his car, Frank's own elbows just inches above the contorted body of Reddeer entombed in the trunk.

"Probably figured you and Karl would vouch for him since he's blood," one of the cops added in an unexpected but fitting dénouement to Frank's tale.

"And when we told him we wouldn't, nothin' to do but come out here and take a bullet like a man," Frank concluded with an air of *The End.*

Just as Karl and Frank's production was about to close the curtain and dim the lights, John Paul Hoff's car pulled in behind the others. He had his own connections at the police department.

Karl steeled himself as Hoff approached, but was surprised by John Paul's calm demeanor and tone when he finally joined the semi-circle around Frank's car.

"Frank. Karl," he greeted both in a flat but nonaggressive voice.

Karl did not respond, but Frank, forever the gamesman, did not hesitate.

"If it weren't for the boys in blue here, Johnny, I'd drag you off this property with one hand."

John Paul ignored him, casting his gaze to Christoph lying there in a state of creeping rigor mortis.

"Is that the son of a bitch who violated my daughter?" he asked rhetorically, before stepping forward to begin kicking Christoph's body as hard as he could.

John Paul drove his Wingtip twice into Christoph's ribcage and was rearing back for a third time when Karl exploded toward him, fists curled and swinging, landing multiple blows before John Paul fell to the ground. The cops restrained Karl as John Paul pulled himself to a standing position once again, wiping the blood dripping from his nostrils with the back of his hand.

"A family of animals. Animals," spat from Hoff's lips before he turned and walked back toward his car, Frank's final words to him echoing off the cabin's wooden exterior.

"It's a dog eat dog world."

CHAPTER FORTY-NINE
Williston, North Dakota (1947)

Harlan's two old farm dogs waited at the top of the drive as they always did when he was away. Two days had passed since Elsie had returned from town to find blood in the kitchen, her father missing. Patrolman had come and gone asking all matter of questions over the past forty-eight hours, but the answers she had offered seemed empty to her now, as empty as the large farmhouse she found herself alone in; scared and confused in the absence of her father who had always been ever-present. *What will become of me?* she thought, but there was no answer to be divined. Their house was the most isolated in the area and she felt as though maybe it was she who had disappeared and that somewhere life went on, somewhere there was laughter, song, discussion, somewhere her father was smoking his pipe as he often did in the evening, somewhere with a new wife, a new family. The thought temporarily alleviated the pressure that had been pressing down on her chest since she had come home to a future now so uncertain. It filled her at once with sadness and hope for it meant that somewhere her father was alive.

The endless expanse of wheat waved in the wind outside the window waiting to be harvested. Seeing it she was overcome and began to cry again; the spirit of her father waving goodbye was all she could see beyond the pane dividing the glass in two reflecting the division now running through her own young life: with her father and without him.

CHAPTER FIFTY
Williston, North Dakota (2011)

Williston cops were everywhere along with North Dakota 'staties' as the locals referred to them. Charlie could see them standing around in his father's front yard, their patrol cars littering the driveway and the shoulder of the highway approaching it. Charlie pulled his truck behind the furthest patrol car parked along Highway 1804 and got out. The walk toward the home where he had grown up and toward the father he still had so much left to say to was surreal. This was not what he had envisioned as their final meeting.

Inside the Cummins Energy trailer where Wendell had offered him a job just two days before, he had been informed that there had been a "problem" at his father's house, but no one had offered any details if in fact they had any to provide. But Charlie didn't need any details. He had known from the moment Wendell had called on the two-way that his father was dead. The cause was still unknown to him as he made his way across the lawn, but he knew in death that his father had gotten the last word. He produced identification for the state trooper standing guard at the front door and entered the house where time simultaneously stopped and spiraled backward over forty years.

A clutch of cops cluttered the living room. There was a din of voices from the various conversations going on, even a bit of laughter here and there and Charlie, who had found it hard to respect his father all his life, found the scene disrespectful. His eyes found the Hidatsa woman he had seen the day before on the landing outside the house. She was standing off to the side and it was clear from her face she had been crying. Charlie also spotted Benjamin talking with a police officer in the far corner of the room. No one seemed to notice Charlie until he demanded in a loud voice, "Get the fuck out, all of you," and then all eyes were upon him, but his own gaze had fallen to his father's chair where the outline of the old man was still seated beneath an afghan someone had draped over him.

"Take it easy, Charlie," one of the cops said in reply. As he moved across the room, Charlie recognized him as Kenny Hartnett, a pot dealer with a bad attitude he had known from his misspent youth in Williston.

"Shut the fuck up, Kenny. And get all of these people out of my house."

"Your house?" Kenny asked sarcastically, "You haven't lived here in twenty years and from what I've heard you just showed up out of the blue in town a few days ago. The two men were now face to face, practically nose to nose, until the coroner stepped between them and ushered Charlie aside.

"Charlie Lund?"

"Yeah. What?"

"I'm sorry to tell you, your father's dead."

"How? How?"

"His throat was slit."

"You mean someone murdered him?"

"I didn't say that. Why don't we step outside?"

But Charlie brushed passed him, walked over to the chair and pulled the afghan off of Karl. His father's head was drooped to his chest and his flannel shirt was a tie-dye of blood stains.

"Don't touch him," the coroner shouted and in an instant several cops were on Charlie, pulling him away, dragging him as he kicked and flailed through the room and out the front door where two of the biggest police officers struggled to subdue him on the lawn, as he continued to resist and to ignore their repeated requests for him to calm down as they handcuffed him.

The handcuffs cut deep into his wrists when they yanked him to his feet a few minutes later. A burly 'statie' deposited him in the back of a cruiser. Charlie kicked at the windows and threw himself about the interior of it until a very young gentleman in a suit— Charlie could only assume to be a detective—leaned his head into the front window and asked him directly through the perforated, metal barrier between them, "Where were you last night, early this morning?"

The thought immediately came to mind that Shannon was his alibi and Charlie laughed out loud at the irony of it all considering Shannon had been at the house the day before threatening to kill his father.

"I was in the bathroom of the 4 Mile Bar getting a hand job from your mother."

The detective, who looked to Charlie like he should be studying for an algebra test instead of hassling him, remained poker-faced when he concluded their exchange, offering so calmly that it was unnerving, "My mother's dead, Mr. Lund. You'll have to come up with something else."

CHAPTER FIFTY-ONE
Mandan, North Dakota (1947)

Karl approached the Hoff residence. It was late, but there was a light on in the house. He had wrestled with what he might say to Marilyn on the long walk across town. He knocked on the door still not sure what words would come out of his mouth. But there was no answer. With much trepidation he opened the door and entered the informal but tidy house and called out Marilyn's name, but there was no response. He moved through the entryway toward the light coming from the living room. There sitting perfectly still on the couch in a robe, her sightline fixed on some indistinct point in the hallway behind him, was Marilyn. Her hair, which he knew she took great pride in, was matted and hung around her face which no longer held the glow it always had. She was pale and drawn with large black circles around her blue, but glazed over eyes.

"Marilyn," he said softly, tentatively, but she said nothing, seeming to not register his presence.

He moved across the room and reached out a hand toward her shoulder, but before it could land she came to life and grabbed his wrist with a strength that belied her slight frame, biting three of his fingers so hard that he yanked it away in a motion reserved for the touching of a hot stove.

He looked to his hand and then to her, her eyes wild but still not looking at him. And then she began growling like an animal. Karl attempted to breakthrough her apparent psychosis, repeating how sorry he was over and over, but to no avail. And then John Paul Hoff was there, in the room and rushing toward him, hitting him with such force that Karl was knocked to the floor before he knew what had happened. John Paul grabbed the fireplace poker and drew it back and over his head. Karl, on his back, began scrambling away backward on his palms, kicking his heels against the hardwood to gain momentum. Karl got to his feet as John Paul swung down hard and the heavy metal poker met his shoulder just as he had regained his footing. Fire filled his body cauterizing his tongue and though he tried to speak, not a sound came from his mouth. John Paul pulled the poker back, his position like that of a hitter in a batter's box waiting on the next pitch and as he began to swing Karl bolted into the hallway, hitting the wall, before regaining his composure and running out the door and into a night that wouldn't end for another sixty-four years.

*

"The devil's finest trick is to persuade you that he does not exist."
- Charles Baudelaire

*

The last conversation Karl would have with Frank, before four years of silence, took place in the early morning hours of the next day. Karl awoke, feeling sore and suicidal, to the sound of pounding at his front door, a pounding he didn't respond to for some time. When he finally opened the door, there stood Frank. He'd forgotten he'd told Frank he wanted to talk over a "business' proposition, one that would free him to begin a new life to pursue the only penance he believed would relieve his soul of the awful weight of guilt which ironically was the only thing strong enough to hold him bound to this life, this world of blood and lies he himself had fashioned with hands of clay God had granted him for who knew how long.

Over the next two hours, Karl negotiated an arrangement with Frank in exchange for his silence Karl knew was both a trompe l'oeil and a point of leverage he had never held before in his dealings with his older brother. No one would ever have to know that Frank had killed both Reddeer and Christoph, if he agreed to Karl's proposition. If not, then he would go directly to the police and willingly spill everything he knew about the murders, letting the chips fall where they might concerning his own complicity. If Frank went along, as he hoped he would, then Karl would at last be free to move on and leave everything he had once known behind for good. Or so he believed.

At this moment, Karl only wanted to get away from Frank. Marilyn's nightmare at the hands of Christoph had pushed him to the brink of madness, the loss of her love darkened his heart as if it had been cast into the depths of Hell, but, oddly perhaps, it was the murder of a simple farmer from Williston that was weighing even more heavily upon his conscience, suffocating the little that was left of his soul. Penance for his acts, for his part in this Shakespearean tragedy could be his only salvation. And so he made a deal with the devil.

CHAPTER FIFTY-TWO
Williston, North Dakota (2011)

What fresh hell is this? Charlie thought as he sat cuffed in the back of the police cruiser. No one could actually think he had killed his father, but then again his sudden appearance back in town probably seemed suspect to even the most casual observer.

Cuffed and confined, alone with his thoughts, he turned reflective.

Regardless of what their relationship had been, Karl had still been his father and now his father was dead. He had sought freedom for himself these past twenty years, only realizing too late perhaps that real freedom meant confronting his demons, his fears, and his father —not running away as he had. Now he was free from his father in the most absolute of terms and the irony was not lost on him that at this moment of final liberation from the shadow which had never left his side, neither in the Florida sun nor in the rain of Oregon, he sat handcuffed in the kingdom of his tormentor.

All Charlie's selfish, self-pitying cogitation evaporated into air as thin as the connection between him and his father when he spotted two E.M.T. attendants carrying either end of a black body bag to the ambulance where they loaded it into the back, unceremoniously closing the door before driving away west on Highway 1804 toward Williston with sirens and flashing lights, loud and bright—too much for the living, but not enough to wake the dead.

Charlie no longer cared what fate lay in store for him, but he had no more accepted this when the cruiser door opened and he was pulled from the vehicle and freed from the handcuffs.

The young detective, his cheap aftershave riding the prairie wind, made an encore appearance.

"Can't hold you. Wasn't going to. No evidence yet. But you might want to work on that alibi. And I wouldn't think about leaving Williston."

"Wouldn't dream of it," Charlie assured him in the most sarcastic tone he could muster.

Charlie turned to leave knowing he needed to find Shannon to coach her on his alibi which he realized she might not provide if she herself were somehow involved. He was halfway to his truck when Benjamin, slightly out of breath, caught up to him, walking beside him, yesterday's fists exchanged for open palms, talking as much with his hands as his mouth.

"So, when do they read the will? I mean, is it before the funeral, after it? And who does that? A lawyer? A judge?"

"There's going to be an investigation, so it's going to be awhile before they just start handing out your grandfather's money."

"What about the land?" Benjamin pressed as Charlie slid behind the wheel.

"What about it?"

"That'd be in the will too, I suppose."

"I suppose," Charlie speculated, noticing just how much Benjamin looked a lot like him. He felt a paternal pang and before he knew it odd, fatherly words were leaving his mouth. "You need a ride somewhere? Need any money?"

It was an awkward moment for both of them, but an icebreaker nonetheless.

"No, but, uh, thanks," Benjamin stuttered back, before adding, "Sorry about your face."

"That's okay. I'm sorry about yours too."

A minute later, Benjamin still looked confused by the comment as Charlie watched him becoming smaller and smaller in his side mirror—as distant from one another as they had always been.

CHAPTER FIFTY-THREE
Sanish, North Dakota (1947)

Karl had never worked so closely with Frank and it was a bittersweet and brief alliance that spoke to all the good they could have done together if they had always shared the same motives and motivations. But they hadn't, until now. Frank's bloodthirst for money now paid off as did Karl's history of crippling, blind allegiance to his older brother. His loyalty, though, this time would pay personal dividends.

The town of Sanish on the Berthold Reservation would in the decade of construction on the Garrison Dam ultimately come to rest under the man-made lake which would result. The elders of the Three Affiliated Tribes hated Frank, but he knew that money would talk for him on this day when he stood before them in private on the reservation. In return for what was a sizable bribe paid out from the Lund Cement coffers, they unanimously agreed to turn a blind eye to what Frank and Karl wanted to bury in an unoccupied, desolate corner of the reservation.

By the end of the day as light was fading, though, a small audience of children from the three different tribes had gathered and watched as Frank and Karl shoveled dirt over two steel drums in two separate and somewhat shallow, side by side pits. Before driving away in one of the Lund company trucks with Frank, Karl pulled a handful of change from his pocket and distributed the coins among the little hands. He loved children and with Frank behind the wheel on the way home, Karl became lost in a fantasy he had indulged in many times before: to have a family with Marilyn. He would never again think so lovingly of children, not even of his own son, Charlie, who was still twenty years away from being born in a sleepy, little hospital in sleepy, little Williston, North Dakota.

CHAPTER FIFTY-FOUR
Williston, North Dakota (2011)

For old timers, Williston was no longer the sleepy farming outpost of their youth. Many lamented the changes the oil boom had brought to the once close-knit community where the cliché of not locking one's doors at night had passed into a history which had always hinted at the riches lying beneath the ground, but had been paved over and drilled through in favor of a future where the whispers of the basin's potential had become the shouting of an army of oil field workers not just in the fields but all over town; a town unable to keep up with the housing, schooling, and entertainment demands of the out-of-state workers and their families flooding the former Timbuktu of North Dakota.

Crime was now on the rise and overwhelming the tiny police force whose pre-boom idea of keeping the peace meant throwing the harmless and hapless town drunk in a cell once a month until he sobered up enough to go home; mediating the occasional flare ups between neighbors over issues of a pet doing his business on the wrong side of the fence; breaking up beer parties of high schoolers without prospects of heading off to college or of being gainfully employed after graduation. Now there were assaults, rapes, kidnappings, and drug mills to contend with on an almost daily basis.

The town Charlie had known twenty years before now seemed at once wired and tired, battered and bemused, full to the brim of haves and have-nots. There were jobs of course and an influx of capital into the economy that would have been unthinkable without the oil boom, but inequity was already ruling the day and those on the bottom were already rooting for the bust that comes, which always comes, as evidenced by little towns just like Williston dotting Texas and Oklahoma which had once ridden a sea of oil to an ephemeral prosperity before, like Cinderella, watching the Fairy Godmother trappings of it all disappear at some unforeseen, but inevitable stroke of midnight. The town of Williston wasn't exactly divided in two over the oil boom, but just that sense permeated the bars and restaurants of Williston where oil workers sat on one side, disgruntled citizens on the other, and local businessmen and -women somewhere in between the two in a delicate dance between old relationships and new. It was just such a scene that played itself out everyday at the Lunch Box.

After an afternoon of fruitlessly searching for Shannon, Charlie had called it quits. Conversations stopped and eyes darted back and forth toward then away from him as he entered the Lunch Box; only loud and rowdy oil workers who really didn't know him from Adam were oblivious to his presence. The locals on the other hand gave him the once over twice and it was obvious to Charlie they had been made aware of his presence back in town and that word was already spreading about his father. As he stood momentarily paralyzed by the awkward scene, he spotted the Hidatsa woman, he had seen at his father's house. coming out of the Lunch Box restroom. Lana also saw Charlie and, without hesitation, she walked right up to him.

"You are a terrible son," came slowly and pointedly from her lips and as Charlie was thinking of what to say she slapped him hard across the face.

A collective gasp came from the patrons and now even the oil workers who had ignored him were staring and one of them, unable to contain his shock and insensitivity, shouted from a back table, "That dude just got bitch-slapped by some squaw."

Lana spun around and dropped a dead eye on the oil worker who turned back to his food as the Lunch Box filled with anxious muttering.

Charlie was still standing perfectly still in the same spot after Lana had left, his cheek stinging and beet red on one side, when he realized someone was talking to him. It was Bob Mosier from the newspaper sitting in a booth along the windows who continued to exhort him to come and have a seat. Charlie walked the few feet which felt like a city block and then sheepishly slid into the booth across from Bob.

"Holy heck, didn't think this town would ever see your shadow again."

Charlie just nodded. Then Bob dropped his high tone. An era had just passed. The history of Williston had been in part written by Charlie's father. He had been a moneyed man when there was none here, but no one ever would have known it, living simply and keeping to himself as he had for decades. There had always been whispers, *How did a farmer have so much money?* There were plenty of other locals who had had just as much acreage as Karl Lund, but had struggled in the years when wheat was down. Karl Lund had never struggled. But Bob, unlike most locals, knew why. He'd made his money not in the fields, but from the dam. Karl had had some skeletons in his closet that took a little digging to find, but Bob had found them years ago. Bob took journalism seriously though and unlike some of his contemporaries had never taken to slumming it by churning out unflattering exposes or giving himself over to the type of tabloid journalism which had become vogue in the past decade. At any rate, Bob knew a little about the Lund brothers from Mandan, but he had never been one to kiss and tell.

"Sorry about your pop."

After the judgment of so many eyes upon him, Charlie was paranoid. He leaned across the table between them, asking in a whisper, "What? You don't think I killed him?"

Bob Mosier reared back unable to contain a laugh.

"My lord, no. Of course not."

Charlie felt a sense of relief he had not experienced since arriving back in town. It was utterly refreshing. Bob Mosier was salt of the earth.

"It's going to fall to me, Charlie, to write your father's obituary. Anything you'd like me to know about him before I sit down to it?"

It was possible that in his absence that half the town now knew more about his father than he. Charlie felt at a loss, sitting a minute in silence before offering not an epitaph, but something which begged more questions than it answered.

"He had a lot of secrets."

Bob accepted the non-answer with a smile and replied warmly, knowingly, "Sometimes that's all we have, perhaps the only things that are truly our own."

*

Charlie sat a long while after Bob left. They had talked and reminisced. Bob had been gracious with his time and had gone into detail about Williston's boom and how it had in fact not only divided the town, but had transformed it in a way that was hard even for the locals who had experienced it to get their heads around. Bob, ever the diplomat, could see both sides. Without the oil revenue the town would have eventually just blown off the map, but on the other hand the slew of problems that had come with it were not just pitting neighbor against neighbor and family member against family member, but were straining the very fabric of the town's services and fraying the once obvious priorities of those in positions of power now forced to make decisions about the future both short and long term.

It was evening outside though the daylight savings light was still hanging on if by only a thread and so Charlie gathered himself and retraced his steps back out through the little restaurant full of diners who now seemed to not give a damn who he was. He walked around town checking out bars, sticking his head in here and there, looking for what felt right after what had been a long day wrought with conflicting emotions; emotions he now intended to drown. Then he stuck his head inside Whispers.

*

Whispers was a strip joint and the joint was hopping and not exactly the contemplative place he was looking for, although he knew the half-clad, jiggling lovelies would not be a distraction from all he was trying to process. But then he noticed Dawes in the back frantically waving him across the room. The fact was the place was as good or bad as any and there were plenty of bars in Williston these days where a man could unwind; bars slapped up by entrepreneurs in a hurry to relieve the oil field hands of their own personal gold rushes. Guys who a few months before were sitting around in any number of distressed, depressed burgs across the country with absolutely zero chance of landing a job beyond what the fast food industry had to offer, were now working the Williston Basin where the oil industry was putting an average of $100,000 a year into their pockets. But the cash infusion came at a price. Their incomes had gone from zero to sixty in the blink of an eye, but their eyes were bleary and bloodshot from the long hours of manual labor they did at a stretch of seven to ten days in a row before getting a day or two off.

The availability of pills and powders to keep them going was a double-edged sword considering few took advantage of the time off to catch up on sleep and those using still needed to feed their addictions just the same as when they were in the field. It was no wonder that incidents of assault and rape had gone through the roof in Williston in the past few years. Work hard, play hard was an understatement and a more apt description of pharma sales reps at an annual meeting in Hawaii than the oil field toughs inhabiting

Whispers. Before him was not blue collar night at Hooters, but more a meth-fueled rugby match looking for an orgy inside a double-wide.

Charlie waded through the testosterone and an elbow-room-only collection of manhood modelled after Ted Nugent at an NRA convention. A potential for violence and extended sexual frustration had been mixing for hours already with the obligatory hard rock and hard liquor producing a dangerous cocktail. Online reviews of Whispers included a comment from a former dancer at the club who warned, *Do not dance here unless you feel like getting raped.* Charlie had always been able to blend in wherever he went, but by the time he had landed in front of Dawes' table, he knew he had his work cut out for him.

Dawes was the master of ceremonies as usual in his little corner of hell and his minions who sat with him looked like WWE rejects and rehab reality show veterans.

"You're blocking the pussy, dick face. Get out of the fuckin' way," greeted Charlie courtesy of one of Dawes' crew and so he slid against the wall near where Dawes was seated.

Over the din, Dawes attempted to introduce Charlie to the disinterested and drunk assembly surrounding him, shouting, "This is Charlie boy, the guy I was tellin' ya' about."

But disinterest turned to unwanted attentiveness as all eyes at the table turned to Charlie. Then one of the minions spoke directly to him prompting the others to join in.

"Hey faggot, I think you'd do better at one of the truck stops around here."

"Least he ain't competition."

"Hey Rick, you like fat chicks. Get the faggot to talk to a fat chick for you. Fat girls love queers."

"Why don't you get up there and dance, boy?"

Charlie couldn't breathe. He looked to Dawes who grinned, winked at him, and then downed a shot, followed by a mug of beer. Finished, Dawes licked his lips, put his hands behind his head, and moved the tobacco plug in his mouth from one side to the other before speaking directly to Charlie.

"Saw Shannon this morning. Girl sure likes to talk when she gets cranking."

Charlie moved toward Dawes. He could feel his fist curling at his side, but he was stopped short when the largest of Dawes' henchman rose to meet him with a set of paws which hit Charlie square in the chest, pushing him back and into another table of oil workers indistinguishable from the one he had just stood beside. Beer bottles had become bowling pins when his ass hit the table and were now either smashed on the floor or spilled onto the table top and into laps of denim.

"I don't drink with no cock suckers," was followed by laughter, back slapping, and good old boys high-fiving one another as Charlie headed for a nearby backdoor marked *EXIT*. But he did not leave alone.

*

When Charlie woke up, a stray dog was licking his face and he swiped at it lamely with his hand, sending it on its way. He could taste blood in his mouth and it took him a good minute to get from where he lay on the ground to his knees to at last standing unsteadily beneath the glow of a streetlight. White hot pain shot through his head and his torso as he began limping his way back to his truck parked some blocks away. His last memory before he had blacked out was of a voice shouting, "Welcome to Williston, Tinkerbell."

CHAPTER FIFTY-FIVE

Mandan, North Dakota (1947)

*

*"What is happening to me happens to all fruits that
grow ripe. It is the honey in my veins that makes
my blood thicker, and my soul quieter."*

- Friedrich Nietzsche

*

Autumn in Mandan was well past although the calendar still only
said November. Bitter winds swooping in from Canada blew through
a series of gray days which turned to weeks without sunshine. In that
time, Karl saw Frank only once and they did not speak. It was at
Christoph's funeral. Christoph was buried without any fanfare. Frank
had simply met the gravedigger, two men from the funeral home
who brought the casket, and a priest. Frank had his youngest brother
laid to rest right next to their mother, remembering how much she
had doted on her little blonde-haired boy when he was a child.

Over the past few weeks Karl had spent most of his time at the
Corner Bar. Even Butch the bartender could see a sea change in
Karl. And unlike their formerly cantankerous relationship, they now

were friendly toward one another, often spending time just talking in the slow hours before a shift change at the railyard. Butch, it turned out, was a bit of a philosopher and though he, like everyone else on either side of the bridge, knew what had happened to Marilyn and who had been responsible, it did not stop him from offering some perspective, even a few lines of poetry from Whitman or Eliot now and again.

After seeing to Christoph's burial, Frank had thrown himself fully into the business. He was now married to Lund Cement and was determined to see that its progeny form the foundation of a state about to make its way into the 20th century, despite the fact that nearly half that century was already over. Karl, as per their arrangement and in barter for keeping secrets secret, now had nothing to do with the day to day operations of the business and simply had a bank account where his equitable share of any and all profits after taxes were to be deposited for as long as the company remained solvent. Frank had already laid the groundwork for many of the contracts that would come to fruition as the Garrison Dam project gained momentum. Without lifting a finger, Karl would become rich over the next ten years. Very rich. But money would never be a salve for his broken heart, would never compensate for the emotional bankruptcy which would come to define him and his life in the coming decades.

He made a few more attempts to see Marilyn, but without success. And when her father had her committed a couple of months after the incident to the same facility as her mother—North Dakota State Hospital in Jamestown—Karl made efforts to visit her on several occasions, but was turned away each time. He held out hope that he would see her again, sometime, somewhere, but that would never come to pass. In all the time that would unfold without her, he never forgot her and kept tabs on her progress and path through the rest of her life through acquaintances in Mandan who had known them both and had watched their budding romance and its tragic end. When word came the following June that Marilyn had given birth to a baby boy in the same facility treating her for what was surely psychosis, Karl pressed the folks he still had contact with in Mandan for details about the adoption by a farm couple in Fargo. But by then he had put further physical distance between himself and his past, having moved to Williston.

*

John Paul Hoff was also never the same man again after the events of the fall of 1947. He had survived his son's death, his wife's mental demise, but, in the end, could not cope with the unthinkable violation of his daughter. In its terrible wake he foundered and his political influence along with his political aspirations simply faded. Despite opinion to the contrary in Bismarck and Mandan, John Paul knew he was not the good man everyone had often made him out to be. His demons were his own and despite having outrun them for years, in the aftermath of the assault on Marilyn they had gained ground until they had simply overtaken him. Fittingly, he died on the day commemorating the completion of the Garrison Dam, June 11, 1953. At the time of his death, the man whose name had been bandied about as a potential gubernatorial candidate had been reduced to fetching parts and cutting lumber at the hardware store in

Mandan, quietly going about his work, speaking only when spoken to.

CHAPTER FIFTY-SIX
Williston, North Dakota (2011)

Standing in a downpour outside Shannon's trailer sometime well after midnight, Charlie pounded relentlessly on the cheap door, beating it with his fists, kicking it, until after five minutes with no answer he put a shoulder against it, leaned his full weight forward, and pushed on through. Inside it was pitch black; shades all drawn and not a single light source lit. He flicked a switch, but illumination failed to materialize. He tried a nearby floor lamp, but to no avail. Most likely a past due, unpaid bill had resulted in her services being cut, but then he noticed a small digital clock across the room, its display glowing red. The juice was on and it occurred to him that she either couldn't afford light bulbs or had forgone the expense in favor of her habit. The life of a junkie was such.

He proceeded tentatively through the dark, yelling for Shannon to get up as he made his way through the unkempt trailer before falling over some unseen object and hard on the plywood floor beneath the stained and cigarette burned builder's grade carpeting. Relying on touch, he pulled himself up to the kitchen counter and made his way along the hallway as a blind person without a cane might, flicking another light switch along the way which was also wired to a dead end. He found her in the bedroom she used as the master and a sad excuse for one with just a mattress on the floor and clothing strewn about everywhere. It was on the mattress that he made out the outline of her body. At last coming to his own senses after his beating, Charlie thought to use his lighter. He flicked it and held it out from his body. Shannon still had the syringe in her arm, her heroin shooting set up in a Hello Kitty lunch box open and beside her. The anger he had carried with him from the alley subsided for the moment. He pocketed the hot lighter and knelt beside her, placing two fingers to her neck. She still had a pulse. Five minutes later he had her in his truck and was headed for the hospital in Williston.

*

Remarkably, before reaching the hospital, Shannon not only came to but was as lucid as he had seen her since he'd arrived in Williston a few days before. Charlie, knowing there would be more questions than he could answer if he continued on to the hospital, turned the truck around and headed back toward Shannon's trailer. She didn't ask a single question, but mentioned she was hungry and wanted to know when the funeral for Karl would be.

Her demeanor was off-putting. As she rattled on inanely about trivialities, including that she would have to miss some of her favorite television shows because her cable had been shut off, Charlie's anger returned two-fold. She offered no defense, issued no denials when he confronted her about telling Dawes of his homosexuality. In reply, she only asked distractedly, "Oh, did I?" That's when he began in earnest to tear her apart verbally, dressing down every aspect of her pathetic life. Her apathy seemed to thaw during the ride and by the time he told her to get out of his truck and to stay out of his life in front of her trailer she was in tears.

"I'm so sorry," she said, standing in the rain outside his truck before he dropped it into reverse and punched it, careening and sliding out backward through the mud track her drive had become. He did not look at her again, although he sensed she still stood outside the trailer when he took the truck out of reverse and stomped the accelerator, propelling the car up the road, swerving around water trucks headed to frack sites, Cummins Energy trucks just like the one he would be driving for the next ten hours.

CHAPTER FIFTY-SEVEN
Jamestown, North Dakota (1948)

Marilyn was more aware than she let on to the staff. She often wandered the halls wearing the theatrical gaze of a mad woman as a mask. In sessions where she was supposed to talk about her feelings, she would only stare out the window behind the doctor until he ended her mandatory twenty minutes of one-on-one therapy.

Patients were forbidden to enter the rooms of other patients, but that had not kept her from occasionally walking into the room where her mother had been living the past year and a half in a state of delirium, heavily medicated, and generally unresponsive. She sat in a chair by her mother's bed, held her hand, and whispered anecdotes from her childhood and the scattered fond remembrances of their better times together.

Marilyn could not go back to Mandan. Would not. But to show progress would mean an eventual call to her father to come pick her up. She knew she had to keep up the charade until she figured out her heart. The mental trauma of what had happened had not left her, but through prayer she had begun to consider the possibility of forgiveness. Forgiveness for Christoph first, for that would be the hardest to come to. Forgiveness did not mean forgetting. She would never forget what had been done to her; not what had *happened* to her, but what had been *done*. She searched her soul for an answer to a question that had perplexed her the past three months: *What was it that she needed to forgive Karl for?* Surely he had known nothing about what Christoph had in mind the night he came by the house and yet she felt that he was somehow to blame. She held him accountable in a way because had he picked her up at the appointed time, then none of this would have happened. The fact was that while her mind had held onto her anger, her heart had held onto her love for him.

One day while sitting and staring out her window at birds alighting upon and leaving the limbs of an old oak tree, they came for her. Attendants entered the room and grabbed her, pulled her to her feet, and held her arms behind her back as a nurse gave her an injection.

She awoke to a burning smell and a sensation of electricity gripping every extremity so tightly as to make them immobile. Then it stopped. Then she heard a voice say, "Again."

Her body stiffened as the electricity passed through the electrodes taped against her temples and into her. When it stopped, she could feel urine beneath her, taste metal in her mouth. But before another round of voltage could be requested and delivered she mustered the remaining energy within her being and screamed as many times as she could in a row, "I'm pregnant! I'm pregnant! I'm pregnant! I'm..."

But again the voltage came, fixing her eyes, arching her spine in an unnatural way. Twice more she endured the clinical lightning before the electrodes were removed and she was wheeled to her room. The electroshock treatments continued and in June after the birth of her baby boy, he was taken from her arms after being allowed to hold him for fewer than five minutes. A day later she was presented with a series of documents and repeated demands for her to sign them, which she refused to do. Her father came, signed them as her proxy, then took her home. She never spoke to her father again. Though she prepared his meals, washed his clothes, and kept his house, not a word was uttered by her in his presence. She watched in silence as the man she had revered as a child, as a teenager, as a young adult became a shadow of what he had once been. Five years after he brought her home he died in his sleep.

A year after her father's death, she received a letter and a photo of a six year old boy from a couple in Fargo who said they had named him Norman. Little Norman looked happy in the photo, holding a fishing line strung with three little catches between his two small hands. Marilyn had looked at the picture a good long time before deciding in the end that ignorance was indeed bliss and that she would never come to call on the Ehrlich family of Fargo as long as she lived.

CHAPTER FIFTY-EIGHT
Williston, North Dakota (2011)

Having not slept or bathed, Charlie waited, chain smoking in the parking area of Cummins Energy's main site. He had arrived almost an hour early for work, but work was no longer on his mind. His eyes darted back and forth as pickups of every make and model dribbled into the wide and long gravel lot. Finally, the one he was looking for entered and snaked its way along the back row, loud classic rock radio blasting from its open windows. Charlie, who held a Styrofoam cup in his hand, began walking toward the back row.

By the time Charlie reached the back row, Dawes was out of his truck, leaning against it, his face tilted into a shaft of sunlight breaking through the remaining storm clouds. He was already surrounded by three other oil field hands who stood in a semi-circle smoking and laughing; laughing until they saw Charlie approaching.

Dawes turned to see what had taken their attention away from one of his tall tales. He exhaled a long stream of cigarette smoke from his mouth which caught the low, bright light of the morning and resembled the breath of a dragon in a child's storybook. Dawes, still on his high horse from the night before, wasted no time in displaying his new found machismo for a fresh audience.

"Hey there, Cindy, your face don't look so good, but there's some boys driving truck out of Frisco over at the Flying J who still think your ass is pretty sweet."

The field hands behind Dawes chortled loudly.

Charlie kept coming until he stood at the front bumper of Dawes truck. Dawes took a long drag from the generic brand cigarette and left it dangling between his lips as he took a step forward toward Charlie and feigned a punch. Charlie didn't flinch, but spoke in a casual tone that belied the events of the evening before.

Holding up the Styrofoam cup, Charlie asked, "You still need some of my piss for your drug test?"

"You can drink that queer lemonade for all I care, Lund. Use that and they'll tell me I ain't high, but that I do have AIDS."

Dawes pulled the cigarette from his mouth and flicked it, hitting Charlie in the face. But Charlie only smiled a grinning smile before throwing the cup full of piss into Dawes' face, which dripped from his drawn, druggy mug as he spit the dribble of it from his lips.

Dawes spit and spit again and again as he hollered, "I got fuckin' HIV in my mouth, fuckin' HIV…"

The field hands near Dawes had backed off considerably now and Charlie stepped forward and threw the first punch of many, dropping Dawes to his knees. Dawes tried to pull himself up by holding onto the side mirror of his truck, but Charlie continued to pummel him from above and Dawes was unable to get the leverage necessary. Charlie finished by grabbing a handful of Dawes' long hair, using the greasy purchase to yank his head back and forth which hit the driver-side door until Dawes went limp and Charlie released his grip, letting him fall in a blood-spattered clump to the gravel.

There was a large group of day-shifters gathered between the parked pickups staring in disbelief, but not one of them said a word before or after Charlie asked the scruffy looking audience, "Anyone else want their ass kicked by this fag?"

Charlie kicked Dawes for good measure, turned and walked through the lot and on in through the gate to start his day in the water truck as though nothing had happened.

CHAPTER FIFTY-NINE

Williston, North Dakota (1948)

*

"The safest and most suitable form of penance seems to be that which causes pain in the flesh but does not penetrate to the bones, that is, which causes suffering but not sickness."

- Saint Ignatius

*

He'd been here before; twice before as a matter of fact. But it had been almost a year. Would she remember him? He hoped not.

Karl's mother had raised her boys to be God-fearing and penitent. Frank had even been that way, until he came back from the war. The devil had found Frank first, but Karl and Christoph had followed their older brother down into the pit. Christoph had paid with his flesh, Karl with his soul, and Frank not at all. He felt no guilt, no pity, and no remorse. Karl felt all three and so found himself, in June of 1948, standing on the edge of the late Harlan Andersson's property just outside Williston.

The wide blue sky was brushed with just a white cloud or two and the sunshine shone with abundance. Karl could feel its welcome warmth across the skin of his arms and even, he believed, thawing his bones of their winter marrow. For certain, the previous autumn would never fully leave him; his heart held its windswept, fallen leaves. But here in summer's cauldron, the sweat beading on his brow felt like a proper crown of thorns he could humble himself to wear. This would be his new life. This would be his penance.

He would court the daughter of the man whose fate had been sealed by nothing more, nothing less than another man's avarice. Karl bore that cross and knew he would until he too drew his last breath, but to at least begin to atone for his sins he would lean on the faith, hope, and charity of a young woman in a farmhouse; a young woman unaware her future husband, the man who would take care of her now that her father was gone, was just outside on the her little country road—not a road to redemption, but one to repentance.

In the coming months he would see her in town from time to time—at the butcher shop, in the bakery, on the street. He would see her, but she wouldn't see him. She might look his way, but she didn't *see* him. But Karl's appearance had changed in the year since he had come calling to convince her father to sell his substantial land holdings. He had lost a lot of weight since then, his appetite severely diminished; an empty stomach to match his empty heart. Always clean-shaven since it had become necessary to take the razor to his face, he now sported a bushy mustache consistently complimented by a few days stubble. And he had spent much time in the sun since spring, walking everywhere and anywhere to enable reflection, to foster contemplation. In short he looked like the farmer he was hoping to become. After a time of chance passings in Williston, it was clear Elsie did not recognize Karl and when he was sure it was so, he made his move.

The courtship began subtly but surely with the last but most opportune of his serendipitous encounters with her. It was near the end of August at the feed lot where Karl worked to pass the days and also where he had procured a small room to rent in the big house on the property. Bags of feed were paid for at the counter inside the barn, but were claimed around back from a hired hand who shoveled feed into burlap sacks and tied them off with twine. That hand on the day Elsie came to purchase chicken feed was none other than Karl. When Elsie got out of her late father's pickup truck, Karl took the opportunity to turn on just a touch of the old Lund charm as he loaded the bags into the truck bed. He told a corny joke. She laughed. He commented on the weather. She concurred. He opened the cab door for her. She nodded her appreciation. He closed the cab door. She offered him a dollar tip. He demurred and counseled her to save it for a rainy day. She sighed slightly and said she'd had her share already to which he replied, "Sorry to hear that, ma'am.," before watching her drive away. But all through that September Elsie came for more feed than she had in the previous three months and one day when Karl had taken off to drive back to Mandan to do some Lund Cement banking, Elsie had asked his replacement where he was. His replacement, another hand named Connie Peters, let Karl know about it and chided him for a week about her. By autumn Karl's penance began in full when he asked her to the movies and she accepted. He was quietly satisfied his concerted if calculated efforts had paid off and was certain he'd never seen a girl eat that much popcorn.

CHAPTER SIXTY
Williston, North Dakota (2011)

Charlie drove the water truck back and forth between different frack sites all morning waiting for the crackle of the two-way with Krouthammer on the other end telling him to get his ass over to the personnel trailer. And just before noon it came.

He sat in the same chair he had the day Krouthammer had offered him the job. Again, Charlie lit a cigarette and waited as Wendell shuffled papers and groaned to himself about this and that, the daily headaches of a man in charge of a zoo full of monkeys. Charlie was waiting to be fired, knew it was coming, so he relaxed and looked about the tiny trailer office. A rodeo calendar. A golf ball in a bottle. A fly strip with no vacancy hanging from the ceiling. A picture of Wendell's chubby wife and an Elvis Presley impersonator in Las Vegas. All the usual trappings of middle management.

Lost in his survey of how the other half lives, Charlie was taken by surprise when two men, dressed in suits no less, and Dawes, entered the tiny room. Krouthammer came to attention though he stayed seated behind his desk. Dawes, bandaged here and there about the face and head, was offered the only other chair in the office and slumped down in it as low as he could go. He shot a sideways glance at Charlie and mouthed the word *faggot* before pulling a pack of Marlboro from his shirt pocket and shaking a butt into his mouth. Oddly, one of the suits produced a lighter from his pocket offering a light which Dawes obliged. Then one of the suits spoke.

"You two have got good jobs. Dawes, you need to lighten up on the dope. Lund, well, I'll get to you. The short take on what happened in the parking lot is this, neither one of you is going to be fired. That edict comes from someone over my head. I'm just the messenger. Secondly, Dawes, you're going to be moved to a crew on the south end of the play to ensure you two frat boys don't run into each other on site anymore. What you do in town on your time off is your business as long as it doesn't involve the law. Okay, Dawes, that's it for you. Wendell will radio you your new detail this afternoon."

Dawes rose to his feet, dropped his lit cigarette on the floor and tamped it out with the heel of one of his work boots.

"This is fuckin' bullshit, man."

"Maybe so, but you're as good a derrick hand as we've seen on any play and we're willing to protect that investment," the talking suit flattered back.

And then there were four. The two suits, the one who talked and the one who hadn't yet, Krouthammer, and Charlie. The talking suit closed the door and began talking again. He motioned to the suit who had remained silent thus far.

"Charlie this is Owen Harris. He's a longtime friend of you father's. He's also his lawyer. I'd like to let him fill you in on a few things."

Owen lowered himself onto a corner of Krouthammer's desk, leaned in toward Charlie and spoke for the first time since entering the room.

"First let me offer my condolences. Your father was an important part of this community for many years. He was generous and available to so many of Williston's residents. I not only worked for him, but I admired him as well. I drew up his will years ago, but he recently changed it. He paid me well to make those changes though I thought the changes were foolish. I can't guarantee what's in this amended will won't be challenged in court, but the long and short of it is he bequeathed all of his property to you, but most of his money to the Three Affiliated Tribes except for a nice little chunk he set aside for that Hidatsa woman who cared for him the past ten years. I am assuming that if your alibi holds tight for the night he was, excuse me, murdered, then you will own the largest untapped acreage in the Williston Basin. In exchange for the rights to drill that acreage, Cummins Energy is prepared to offer you a very generous lease agreement which would allow you to continue on in the house you grew up in. They are also prepared to offer you a position on their board of trustees which comes with all of the usual fiscal and community status fringe benefits one would expect from such an appointment. Not that you'll need either should you choose to lease the land exclusively to Cummins Energy." Then he finished with a wink, saying, "You see, Charlie, I work for many clients, your late father among them."

Charlie had lived a little bit in the past twenty years since leaving Williston and he had a nose for a rat. He was taken aback by the frank talk of Mr. Harris, but at the same time it was a relief that his father's large estate was being handled by a professional. No games, just business. But more than intuition said Mr. Harris also had a foot in the Cummins camp, which meant there was probably an angle Charlie wasn't seeing yet. At this point, though, it was better to play along.

"I'll have to think about it, Mr. Harris."

"Of course you do, Mr. Lund," Harris agreed, but added in the same breath, "There's only one complication and my firm is looking into it."

"What's that?" Charlie asked.

"It seems the land is bequeathed to you, but the profits of any lease or sale of it must be shared with a gentleman by the name of Norman Ehrlich. We're trying to track him down."

Charlie's father had taken most of his secrets to the grave with him, but it seemed to Charlie that even in death his father was refusing to play it straight.

The meeting at which Charlie assumed he was going to be fired, but which instead shed light that was going to be hard for him to ignore, had come to an end. But as he rose to shake hands with the assembled, a foreman entered the room without knocking.

"There's been an explosion. It's near that same area where we had the methane gas migration issue last fall. There's a structure on fire. No word on fatalities or injuries, but we know a woman lives in the trailer they are trying to put out."

CHAPTER SIXTY-ONE

Garrison, North Dakota (1948)

Frank was hitting his stride. After a few years of positioning Lund Cement as a regional player in Bismarck and Mandan, he had upped his investment in the business by funneling profits back into it; something his father had never done with any regularity. His old man had been content to do sidewalks on either side of the river, but Frank had seen the potential of the company while still doing finishing work on those same sidewalks. He viewed his time on his knees smoothing concrete as a metaphor for his position in life at that point. Years beyond those days, with dozens of contracts in hand for the Garrison Dam project and dozens more coming, he stood tall in a state about to make the great leap forward.

Frank knew to make money, money had to be spent, so he poured big bucks into a move that would make him a bonafide player in the construction of the dam: moving the bulk of the business to the town of Garrison just north of the dam site. It also enabled him to leave Mandan behind, the geography where he had struggled to make something of himself. He went back less and less and enjoyed it not at all when he did. The sycophants at the Elks turned his stomach anymore and he avoided Bismarck whenever possible when he returned to the area. They were saps stuck in dead end jobs, selling insurance or working in management for the Burlington Northern Railroad in Mandan and hoping for, dying for a transfer to the headquarters in St. Paul, Minnesota. Frank hated depending on others. He was a self-made man in a post-war era that was pushing conformity and corporate allegiance.

He was also now a free man; free from the inconvenient entanglements of married life after Eleanor filed for and was granted a divorce at the beginning of the year. They remained friendly mostly because the alimony arrangement had been generous. Frank loved and led the life of a bachelor. He had an ostentatious house built on significant acreage just outside Garrison and even hired the contractor who put in the swimming pool at the Flamingo in Las Vegas to build him an exact replica in what had been a wheat field, but was now Frank's backyard.

The Flamingo had opened the year before in 1947 and Frank had first gone there over the past winter to get away from the whispers around Mandan and Bismarck that he had more than a little blood on his hands. Frank was smitten with Las Vegas and had been back twice since. Where once he had his eyes solely on the promise of oil out near Williston, he now had dreams of opening his own casino in the desert. During the summer of 1948, it was not uncommon to see B-list movie actors and actresses sitting around his plains oasis shivering their tales off in swimsuits that were no match for the winds across the plains. Frank who had always gambled in business had acquired a taste for the real thing; a handle in one hand, a free drink in the other, and cocktail waitresses in his room at the

Flamingo. And it was only now that he was about to begin making real money with the dam project in full swing and his cement trucks rolling. The future looked bright, but it was only a mirage.

Frank rarely thought of Karl anymore. His only connection to him was the financial arrangement they had made in return to keep secrets secret. He knew Karl had finally played him, but life was good with plenty to go around. Besides, he'd taught Karl everything he knew. But now his brother was nothing more than a bank account number he filled out on deposit slips. He had heard through the grapevine that Karl was living in Williston and working at a feed lot. Karl's lack of ambition reminded Frank of their father. He was happy to have free reign over the business and if Karl got rich as a result too, that was just the price of doing business. He didn't need Karl, never had. But unbeknownst to him, he would. Fate was already conspiring to bring them back together one last time.

CHAPTER SIXTY-TWO
Williston, North Dakota (2011)

By the time Shannon's trailer had been put out, there was nothing but a blackened base left. It smoldered while the wind whipped threads of smoke up and away into the blue sky in full bloom over the prairie. Two fire trucks, an ambulance and a paramedic vehicle made up only four of the vehicles surrounding the burnt out shell. A dozen other vehicles all had the same Cummins Energy logo emblazoned across them with the company's catchphrase in a green, italic font: *Tomorrow's Energy Today*. Shannon had always lived for today, but tomorrow would no longer be in her future.

After Charlie had left her there standing in the rain outside her trailer, she had gone inside to have a good cry. And she did, but not for long when she remembered her Hello Kitty lunch box, wondering if Charlie had done anything with the few jacks she knew she had left before passing out. She could never bring herself to use the word overdose. Despite her perilous, reckless lifestyle, Shannon had always feared death.

Her stash intact, she had proceeded to shoot up twice. As the heroin began its sleepy magic on her system, she made her way unsteadily to the living room couch. Her cigarettes were there on the coffee table and, though she normally only ever smoked outside the trailer because of the fumes inside, she pulled one from the pack, put it to her chapped lips and lit it. The fireball was enormous and the heat so intense that when her body, a mummified charcoal, was taken to the coroner, it had to be identified through dental records.

Bob Mosier stood about a hundred feet from what was left of the trailer. He'd already made the rounds, asking emergency personnel and all the gathered Cummins Energy representatives for a statement. All had politely declined. His thoughts turned to Charlie who would now bury his father and his wife in the same week. *God damned oil*, he thought. The oil robber-barons as he thought of them had hounded Karl to death the past two years trying to secure drilling rights on his vast spread. Their fracking, with its inevitable methane migration, had most likely been the murder weapon which had brought about Shannon's horrific death. He'd finished writing Karl's obituary the night before and knew what was on his plate for tonight. Bob was close to finishing an exposé on the oil boom in Williston which painted an unflattering picture. Its working title was *For a Fistful of Dollars*. He had borrowed it from his favorite Clint Eastwood movie. But this was no movie, this was reality: a dead woman and no one held accountable. Williston, he believed, was trading its future for a fistful of dollars and its inequitable distribution. One day the oil would be gone and all that would be left would be a ghost town full of unwed mothers, alcoholic and addicted men, abandoned housing, and rampant unemployment.

There was nothing to be gained by sticking around. No one would be talking. It was company policy to say as little or nothing if possible; and as far as the emergency personnel, they were as much in the pocket of Cummins Energy and the other various oil companies working the basin as the police and politicians around Williston. He walked to his beat up, 1999 Subaru, got in and drove home to write an obituary for the second night in a row.

*

The sun was going down, bathing Charlie's already tinged face in a vibrant orange. He watched the yellow police tape surrounding the remains of Shannon's trailer whipping in the wind. He'd already been sitting in his truck for about two hours, just staring, his mind blank, his punching bag heart deflated inside his sunken chest. *All the money in the world*, he thought. Shannon would be the third person he would have to bury in the past year.

The prairie looked electric in the sunset. It was beautiful, it always had been, but now it was littered with oil rigs and derricks almost anywhere the eye could wander. It looked unnatural to him, but he would have to decide whether or not he would lease his father's land, whether he too would participate in the madness that had swept the town into the future which was now a present full of drugs, derelicts, and death. What would Williston's future look like after the future had come and gone? It was grim and he wanted no part of it, but his father had roped him in good. Charlie was sure the old man was chuckling, perhaps not in Heaven, but somewhere.

A little car coming down the road slowed, pulled off the highway and stopped only when it was bumper to bumper with Charlie's truck. Behind the wheel was Benjamin. He stepped out and stared in the direction of the smoldering ruin that had once been his home.

Charlie got out of his truck and walked over and stood beside him. He put an arm around Benjamin's shoulder and pulled him close. Benjamin did not flinch away and they both just stood and stared into the distance until the sun disappeared. They did not speak, until finally Charlie said, "How about a beer?"

"Sounds good."

CHAPTER SIXTY-THREE

Las Vegas, Nevada (1951)

The atmosphere in the cigar-smoke-choked private room in the Flamingo Hotel had turned desperate for Frank. He had been sitting in the same chair for the past three hours and was down to his last thousand dollars in chips; down to his last thousand dollars period.

"Let's take a break," Frank propositioned to the circle of high rollers at the table.

There was grumbling, but in the end it was agreed to take a fifteen minute break. Bladders were full of complimentary cocktails and everyone headed to the lavatory but Frank. Frank made a beeline to the cashier he knew best sitting in utter boredom behind his cage.

"I need a ten thousand dollar advance, Joey."

"Can't do it, Mr. Lund."

"You can and you will you fucking glorified busboy," Frank shouted at him, spittle from his lips now dripping down the bars.

"I'll be right back, Mr. Lund."

Frank lit a cigarette and lifted a cocktail off a passing waitress's tray without her noticing. He didn't know what it was, but he downed it just the same.

A few minutes later a manager in a suit appeared behind the bars of the cage.

"Good evening, Mr. Lund. Unfortunately, the Flamingo is unable to grant your request. You have already taken two advances against what I am not sure, but you have reached your credit limit with this establishment."

Frank pressed his face against the bars and in a voice which got the attention of both the slot players behind him and two security thugs fresh from Bayonne, New Jersey, he yelled at the manager, demanding "You will. You will give me an advance. I've been coming here for three years. The money I've dropped here has probably bought half these new slots. Gimme ten grand now or I'm gonna make sure you don't make it to your car when your shift is over."

*

Frank pulled himself to his feet. Tourists filed past him on the sidewalk. He brushed himself off and noticed both the elbows of his tailor-made suit were torn. He had kicked and shouted obscenities the entire way out of the casino as the two goons had dragged him through the slots area and thrown him to the ground outside the entrance. Both still stood there, arms crossed across their chests, blocking any possible entry back into the casino.

In Frank's suit pocket was all he had left: a plane ticket back to Bismarck, North Dakota. Over the past thirty-six months he had gambled away everything he had worked for. Lund Cement was in shambles, the dam contracts dried up, and his dream of opening his own casino in tatters just outside the one where he had gambled away his future.

A sliver of hope was still a few months away. In April, he would renew his dream of being a major player in North Dakota, but here outside the Flamingo, it was neither an option nor a thought.

CHAPTER SIXTY-FOUR

Williston, North Dakota (1951)

Four years into his arrangement with Frank, Karl was a wealthy man. He had more money than he would need in a lifetime. But he had watched his parents struggle during the depression, had seen families fall apart during that era and so he continued to manage his assets. After marrying Elsie in 1949, he had taken over the day-to-day management of her father's farm which was already the biggest in the county. He invested his new and gushing spring of capital from Lund Cement's lucrative dam contracts into new equipment, better technologies, and continued expansion. His land holdings in and around Williston were ten times as large as his nearest competitor and his bankroll allowed him to hire the best hands in the area because he was able to offer a wage well above what others could. Karl had even bought the feed lot where he had first worked when he arrived in Williston.

But cracks had begun to show in his arrangement with Frank and it worried him, despite his tidy fiscal house and smart investments. After Frank missed the first two monthly deposits for the year, Karl tried to reach Frank repeatedly, calling up to Garrison where Lund Cement had been headquartered since 1948. Each time he called he was told by a secretary that Frank was in Las Vegas. This, Karl knew, was not just a potential problem, but a possible disaster in the making.

Though he had uneasy feelings about what he knew concerning Frank's flights of fancy, he could never have imagined just how south everything had gone in Garrison. The many contracts for the dam and its manifold ancillary projects had become but a few now and even those were being frittered away as Karl worried and Frank squandered. The bulk of the contracts for providing cement, labor, equipment and oversight had been lost in one fell swoop when a government auditor discovered he'd been double billing for almost two years. Lund Cement was actually in litigation with Uncle Sam who wanted his money back. Meanwhile, Frank had been robbing Peter to pay Paul. He had, over the past year or so, begun to charge huge upfront fees to new clients which he then used to pay off those he was in debt to, leaving no money to complete the job he had not even started. Worse yet, he was taking a substantial cut of those upfront fees to keep himself in the lavish lifestyle he had become accustomed to and to feed his gambling habit. Karl was already having sleepless nights without knowledge of any of Frank's pecuniary shenanigans.

His marriage to Elsie was pleasant but not passionate by his choice not hers. He didn't love her, he was obligated to her. But still, it was not an unpleasant penance and he felt good that he could do his part to ensure the welfare of the daughter of the man whose death he had set in motion. Maybe, just maybe, Heaven would have room for him when his time came if he could stay the course. Elsie was neither happy nor unhappy. Their marriage was more of an arrangement, just like the one he had with Frank, only Elsie was doing a better job of holding up her end than his older brother.

There were still attempts on Karl's part to see Marilyn. After marrying Elsie he had tried to make a clean break, but he was weak and his love remained for the woman he knew he'd always love. On two separate trips back to Mandan, he had parked outside her house, hoping she would happen to walk out the door. She hadn't on either occasion and he was unable to muster the courage to just knock. Though he was now hundreds of miles and four years away, he could not escape her. Once in Williston, he noticed a woman the spitting image of Marilyn walking down the sidewalk away from him as he drove, but before he could glimpse her face he rear-ended another vehicle. As the driver was berating him, all Karl could do was crane his neck to see past the man's rather large head only to see that the woman had disappeared either around a corner or into one of the stores along the street. He would be twenty-nine this year and wondered how a man of his age could be so lovesick. For all of his very adult financial achievements, Karl was in some ways still a teenager stuck in the throes of puppy love.

CHAPTER SIXTY-FIVE

Williston, North Dakota (2011)

*

"Mostly it is loss which teaches us about the worth of things."
- Arthur Schopenhauer

*

The two funerals could not have been more different. Karl's was standing room only in St. Joseph's Parish. People came from every corner of the state to attend. The Three Affiliated Tribes sent a delegation decked out in traditional dress and were permitted by the church to perform a short, but very beautiful song sung in the Siouan language of one of the tribes and accompanied by a dance around the casket. Karl had been generous to so many in his lifetime and they had not forgotten. The eulogy was delivered by Dick Tuttle, a longtime hand on the farm who had worked for Karl for the past thirty years. Others spoke as well and as they did, Charlie wondered to himself who they had come to bury, certainly not *his* father. At the same time, he began to understand things about his father he never had through the words of these men and women, who in some cases were complete strangers to him. He had been a terrible son.

The day was another stunner in a series of stunners during the past week. Spring was well underway at last here in this northwest corner of North Dakota and in drenching sunlight outside the church, Charlie must have shaken hands with two hundred people after the funeral had concluded.

On the other hand, because of her complete lack of affiliation with any organized religion over the course of her adult life, Charlie thought it best to accept the undertaker's offer at the Fulkerson Funeral Home on West Highland to have a small service right there. It was attended only by Charlie and Benjamin. Afterward, Shannon was laid to rest in Riverview Cemetery.

Karl's will was very specific in the details of his funeral and burial. So, after the service concluded, Charlie and Benjamin followed behind the hearse in Charlie's pickup as it made the long trip to Mandan where Karl was laid to rest the following day beside Christoph in Mandan Union Cemetery.

It was on the long drive back from Mandan that Benjamin asked about the will again and Charlie finally related what it had detailed concerning the distribution of the estate. Benjamin did not take it well. The last half of the drive was completed in silence.

*

Charlie sat for a long time in his father's chair after arriving home to the house he'd grown up in which was now his. He reflected on the funerals and on the decision which had to be made. Cummins Energy, their lawyers, and his father's lawyer had been pressing him the past week for an answer concerning their offer. He asked his father for guidance in a whisper to the ceiling and when he awoke in the same chair the next morning he knew at once what he had decided. He had lost so much in the ten days he'd been back in Williston, but he'd also found something out about himself: he was his own man, not just his father's son. His decision was his own. Tomorrow he would drive to Fargo. The Cummins' lawyers had found the Norman Ehrlich named in his father's will and legally he needed this man's permission to put in motion his plan for the future.

CHAPTER SIXTY-SIX
Garrison, North Dakota (1951)

Frank no longer left his palatial house which had fallen into disrepair as a result of his financial problems. Night after night he stewed trying to think of a way out; sleeping most of the daylight hours away as a natural consequence. The work on the Garrison Dam continued on without him or Lund Cement and the projected finish date of the summer of 1953 was now within shouting distance after four years of construction. February and March of 1951 did not so much as see Frank's shadow after his return from Vegas, broke and broken, but in early April, a Lund Cement project manager still loyal, stopped by to check on him. They talked about the dam, about the weather, and about shifting the focus of Lund Cement to smaller city and rural projects, such as housing foundations and, much to Frank's distaste, sidewalks. Just before the project manager left, he jokingly quipped that maybe the oil industry could be a potential client now that oil had just been found in Williston. Frank's eyes opened wide for the first time in months as he pressured the project manager to remember any details he could about the find. After he left, Frank showered and shaved for the first time in a week, put on his best suit, and stopped in town for a haircut before setting out for

Williston. He needed to talk with Karl, the largest land owner in Williston. And why shouldn't he, this had been Frank's idea all along, hadn't it?

CHAPTER SIXTY-SEVEN
Williston, North Dakota (1951)

Elsie had recognized Karl right away the first time she passed him on the street in Williston, but she had pretended not to. He was the man who had wanted to buy her father's land. She had continued to remain aloof to who he was as they continued to cross paths in the summer of 1948. But when she went to the feed lot to purchase chicken feed that day three years before, she had done so because she knew he worked there. His face had changed. He looked older as she stood face to face with him for the first time again. There was a sorrow, a loss in his face she could not fully define but it was there. It was as though he had aged ten years in just one. But he remained handsome. She had been smitten with him from the first. There seemed to be a gentleness to him, an understanding nature that even when her father turned him away on both occasions, the final time with a shotgun in his hands, this man had shown a depth of character which surprised and impressed her. Now, married to him for the past two years, it was he who was aloof.

Though he provided for her, managed the farm for her, and tended to all matters financial, he was often distant now, as though he were still living in the world he left behind when he came to court her. And she knew he had come to court her. Often while running errands in town before they began dating, she would turn to find him looking at her, whether through a shop window or cattycorner on the street. He was so obvious when he thought he was not, that it was pathetic, but also very sweet. His appearance was all man, but his demeanor had been that of a teenager with a crush. She had found the combination irresistible. She knew almost right away after Karl showed up in Williston in the summer of '48 that she would marry him.

Her father had never been found and the pain of that she bore in her heart to this day. She had long since accepted that he was dead and the police had long since given up trying to find out his fate. A year ago, she buried the past with Karl's help; picking a plot available next to her mother, his wife; choosing a headstone; procuring a coffin and burying it in a hollow ceremony with only a priest and the gravediggers in attendance with her and Karl to watch the empty casket lowered into the ground.

She still kept her weekly vigil, spring through fall, bringing a clutch of fresh wildflowers to her parents' graves, clearing the wilted bunch she had left the week before, placing the new pauper's bouquet in their place, and staying a while to pray in both English and her mother's native tongue.

Her father had been the most beloved man in Williston though he was soft spoken and often aloof. It seemed to her, that Karl was becoming him; neither tender nor terrible; neither emotionally available nor unromantic. He was as even of a man as she had ever come across which is why the events of Friday April 11, 1951 both shocked her and stayed with her to her deathbed, though she never spoke of them to Karl, nor to anyone else.

*

That morning began like any other weekday morning. There was breakfast to be made, dishes to be cleaned, and clothing to be washed. Karl rose early as he always did and began his ritual of tending to the needs of the livestock; milking, feeding, herding them on horseback to the area where they grazed the day away. He worked through the day with his most-trusted, salaried hand who came each day to help keep the large farm running smoothly. By the evening he had settled into his favorite chair to read as he always did, the cat curled on his lap. He often fell asleep in the chair, sometimes coming to bed when he awoke in the middle of the night, but most often not anymore, instead sleeping the night through until morning in that same chair.

It was just after eight in the evening when she and Karl were both rousted from their usual activities by a persistent pounding at their front door. Karl rose to his feet and made his way out of the room. As he passed through the main hallway, he stopped and looked to Elsie in the kitchen who stood at the sink looking back at him, a potato peeler in one hand, a spud in the other. He held a hand up for her to stay put and then walked on. There was a loaded shotgun in the small coat closet by the front door, but Karl didn't give it a thought as he went to open the door, figuring it was a neighbor from down the road with a sick calf or a stuck tractor who needed a hand, things Karl was always amenable to helping out with no matter the hour.

Karl hadn't seen Frank in almost four years and he was taken aback by his appearance when he opened the door and found his older brother standing there. Frank looked awful. His normally robust build had withered and he was as skinny as Karl, something Frank had never been. Frank's eyes were hollow but wild and though he had a good suit on, it was ill fitting probably due to his weight loss. It hung on him the way an old work shirt hangs on a scarecrow after it's been in the elements all season.

Before Karl could even greet him, Frank was off to the races, frenetic, and talking a mile a minute.

"I got it all figured out. Why didn't you call me? This is big news. We have to be positioned just right. Garrison's a wash, the dam's almost done. The only question is where to relocate in Williston. I figure with your spread, it might be smart just to have it here, but that's just a detail. Can I come in? Damn cold out here you know."

Before Karl could answer, Frank brushed past him and they both were standing in the corner.

"Slow down, Frank. What the hell are you talking about? And, why haven't you made the deposits? It's been three months."

"That's chump change, Karl. Just like you to be focused on a songbird in a tree when there's a flock of pheasant at your feet. You'll get you three months' worth out of my share, don't worry."

"The business is washed up from the inquiries I've made. What share? What the hell are you talking about and why are you here?"

"I heard you married the Andersson girl? Where is she? Congratulations. That was my idea, you know…"

Karl grabbed Frank by his necktie cutting him off in mid-sentence. He twisted the expensive silk tight in his hand. Karl was the strong one now. After what had amounted to almost three years of continuous, hard physical labor, Karl was fit and powerful. Without his former bulk, Frank no longer held an advantage.

Karl pulled him in close and whispered in his ear, "Keep your god damned voice down. Now, tell me why you're here before I throw you out."

Frank had never been in this position with Karl. His brother was stronger than he'd ever seen him and so he whispered in return, repeating himself with one simple word, "Oil. Oil. Oil."

Karl released his grip and he and Frank whispered back and forth for a few minutes.

"What oil, Frank?"

"Oh, don't play dumb. This was my idea and now it's happening. Heard all about it. They discovered oil down here in Williston and most likely with your spread we're sitting on a fortune little brother."

"You're crazy. I'm a farmer. I have no interest in oil or anything else for that matter. Now get out of my house."

With those words the old Frank materialized right before Karl's eyes.

"I don't think so, Karl. This land is as much mine as it is yours. Now where's that little Indian girl you been sleeping with? I got a story to tell her."

And with that, Frank turned and started down the hall, but for once in his life Karl did not hesitate and moved after him, swiping one of two brass candlestick holders from the small, scallop-detail hall table as he caught Frank from behind. He struck Frank directly in the back of the head with a heavy blow and Frank crumpled to the floor.

Karl bent over and grabbed Frank by the collar of his jacket and flopped him over onto his back, the candlestick holder pulled back above his shoulder and coiled to deliver another blow; but it wasn't necessary. Blood from the gaping head wound was already seeping out around the edges of Frank's head. Karl, the candle holder still tight in his fist, felt eyes upon him and he looked up from Frank to see Elsie, her head peeking out from behind the doorjamb of the kitchen, her mouth hanging open in disbelief.

"What have you done?"

Karl's usually easy demeanor changed instantly.

"Go to bed. This didn't happen. And you will never say a word about it again. Do… you… understand?"

She looked at him a moment, looked to the body lying lifeless in their foyer, and looked to Karl again, finally answering him, "Yes, Karl."

"Good. Now go to bed. I'm going to take care of this."

She obeyed and took to the steps. She would not sleep a wink the entire night.

Karl knelt down beside his brother after Elsie ascended the steps. He rooted through Frank's pockets until he found his car keys. He knew one man loyal enough and with the means to help him with what he was about to do.

He placed a call to his top hand, Connie Peters, who he had first worked with at the feed lot after arriving in Williston. A half hour later Connie was there and after a long talk over a few whiskeys, they got started.

CHAPTER SIXTY-EIGHT
Williston, North Dakota (2011)

Newspaper in hand, Charlie walked in to the Lunch Box and spotted Bob Mosier sitting in his usual booth. Charlie had been given two weeks off by the brass at Cummins Energy to think over their proposition. Oddly, it was two weeks off with pay which had made Charlie chuckle considering he was sitting on potential millions while he was supposed to be mulling it over.

Bob had done a bang up job on both Shannon and his father's obituaries, but it was the article in this morning's paper which had turned Charlie's head and practically everyone else's in town. The man of the hour was sitting in his usual booth reading, of all things, a copy of *The New Yorker*.

"I ordered for you. Hope you like creamed chipped beef on toast." Charlie didn't.

"This is some article you wrote. Somebody's gonna put a bounty on your head. I better eat at the counter," Charlie joked.

"No, I'm a hack. Now this is a well-written article about what's going on out here," Bob answered, handing the open magazine to Charlie.

Charlie took it and found himself scanning an article entitled *Kuwait on the Prairie* about Williston and the oil boom. He handed it back to Bob and took a seat.

"Yours is better. You really dress down the oil companies, especially Cummins. I just about choked on my coffee when I was reading it this morning. I mean, you've got inside sources, dirt on guys, cover ups, bribes... shit, you left no stone unturned."

"Well, Charlie, it's a little thing I've been dabbling in the past thirty years or so called journalism. I'm thinking, though, my hobby might be getting in the way of my golf game. But this piece in *The New Yorker* is a level way beyond me. You oughta read it. Can't figure out how a guy from New York City could write a better article than me about this deal out here."

"The shit is going to hit the fan I bet," Charlie surmised.

"Don't be so sure. Those oil fellas got a lot of money. They'll probably just buy the paper and fire my ass. Speaking of a lot money, you decided anything yet?"

Two heaping plates of creamed chipped beef on toast arrived at the table. Charlie thought it looked like cat vomit and avoided contact with his silverware on the off chance some of the kitty slop would get in his mouth. Bob dug right in, waiting for an answer.

"As a matter of fact, Bob, I have. I'm going to sign the property over to my son and once that's all legal eagle I'm leaving town."

"I don't blame you. Where do you think you'll go?"

"Never been to Hawaii. No oil there, that's for sure," Charlie answered with a little laugh.

"No snow either. Good choice."

Charlie pushed his plate away and stood up.

"Thanks for breakfast, Bob."

"You mind if I finish what you didn't start?"

"It's all yours, my friend. Let me get the tip."

"Nah, just send me a postcard from Hawaii when you get there. You off to Cummins?"

"Nope. Heading to Fargo to see a man about a horse, Bob."

Bob knew who Charlie was referring to, though Charlie had no idea he did. Bob thought it best to let a man discover on his own what a man might discover.

"Just don't stand behind it. Got kicked once by a Paint working at the Williston rodeo. That's why I walk funny."

Charlie couldn't resist and jumped in with a little self-deprecating humor to end the exchange.

"I walk funny too, Bob, but my story doesn't involve a horse. Take care."

A smile broke across Bob's face and he simply nodded to Charlie who turned and walked out of the Lunch Box.

*

A little while after Charlie left, Bob's cell phone rang. He thought it could be a call canning his ass. He answered. It was, in fact, the editor at *The Herald*. Bob's job was safe, but another obituary was going to be on tap. There'd been an accident on the southern end of the Basin at a Cummins drill site. A derrick hand had been crushed to death while rigging pipe. Bob jotted on a napkin what few details there were including the man's name, *Dawes*, the editor on the other end of the line unable to confirm if it was a last name or a first.

CHAPTER SIXTY-NINE
Williston, North Dakota (1952)

Marilyn wandered around Williston. It had been a long drive and the light was fading in the June sky. It was just after 9 p.m. She'd been walking all over the quaint, if unremarkable, town for two hours, trying to get her courage up. She'd known for a while this was where Karl had ended up, but that was about it. Almost five years had passed since that terrible night in the autumn of 1947 and though the anger had not subsided, she felt it was time to forgive Karl. What part had he played in the entire nefarious affair, if any, was still uncertain to her, but she had carried an odd guilt because she had not let Karl tell his side of the story. She also still loved him which further complicated her mixed emotions.

She asked a passerby if he knew Karl Lund. He said he didn't know him personally, but that everyone knew who Karl Lund was. She asked where she might find him and the man gave her directions that would take her just outside town to the largest farm around Williston. He told her she couldn't miss it, but not to be confused by the name painted across the big red barn in stark white letters: *Andersson*. She could miss it if she never went there was her thought after the man walked on.

It would be totally dark soon, so if she were going to go, she needed to get going.

Marilyn wandered back to her car and headed out of town. As she drove, she thought she might throw up. Her stomach was jumping up and down and wave after wave of nausea hit her. She opened her car window and let in the cooling, late dusk air. She needed to breathe. *Am I really doing this?* she asked herself. She was. And not long after heading out from Williston, she spotted the barn, but didn't stop, driving instead just past the house and parking on the side of the road.

Once she felt it was dark enough, Marilyn exited the car and looked up at the sky which was a crowd of stars, too many to take in and her head moved from side to side as she attempted to recognize as many constellations as she could. At first she spotted only the obvious ones; the Big Dipper, the Little Dipper, and Orion's Belt and such. After a while, when her eyes had fully adjusted, she found the one she was looking for: Andromeda.

It had always been her favorite. She loved the story of the beautiful Andromeda conspired upon by jealous nymphs awaiting her fate, tied to the rocks, the sea monster Cetus about to set upon her with its razor teeth when Perseus, her hero on his winged horse Pegasus, swoops in just in time to save her from a fate not brought on by herself, but by others. This was her story. She had waited for her Perseus to come to her, but he had not, so now she would come to him. It wasn't a matter of forgiveness; it was a matter of love that had delivered her beneath this sky with its diamonds of light, of hope twinkling upon a curtain drawn over Heaven. She had given her soul to God long ago, but she had given her heart to Karl. As she walked up the large front yard toward the house with its three windows lit by lamplight, she felt sure her life would begin again, that seeing his face again would wipe clean the slate between them, and that he would love her as he once had.

She peered through the window at the front of the house which shone with yellow light and saw a dining room with a small a Tiffany lamp on a low hutch, a large table with six round back chairs around it and a corner cabinet which held fine china and crystal glasses. It was a simple but elegant room with tasteful wallpaper. The appointments, though few, she could tell were expensive. They were not typical of the farmhouses she had been in before. Karl was doing well. She always knew he would. Marilyn had always encouraged him to strike out on his own, to make his own way in the world, and to get away from his older brother, Frank. The thought of Frank gave her a chill, though the night air was still warm from a day of full sun in a cloudless sky. Frank had always frightened her, but, still unbelievable to her, it was Christoph who had revealed himself to be a monster behind his boyish good looks and seemingly affable nature.

Christoph alone was to blame for all that had gone wrong for here she was on the outside looking in on a life which should have been hers. She knew Christoph had shot himself. *A fitting end for a coward*, she thought. But though she still lived, he had murdered her too, for all the years since she felt she was among the dead. A spirit haunting a past once more, longing for the connections of the flesh which had been ripped from her delicate hands; hands that had once held Karl's face as she gazed into his eyes glimpsing their future together. It was all within her reach again and so she moved slowly toward the left side of the house where another glowing window waited for her like a crystal ball ready to let her glimpse her future, her love once again.

She could hear the cows in the barn beyond the house chuffing and huffing as she rounded the corner. She stopped short of the window spilling its shafts of light onto the lawn beneath. She held her breath. She let it out. She held it once more and then peeked in the window.

There he was, her Perseus, asleep in a chair, a cat curled at his feet, and an open book in his lap. Karl had always been an intellectual; had read twice as much as she and would rivet her for hours with his knowledge of the world, his sensitive and patient manner for his student both comforting and reassuring. She missed those talks. She spoke with no one now, not even her father, ever. When her father brought her home, none of her friends had come to call and they never did again. She knew how people looked at her. She could feel their pity, and yes, even their contempt for her. Whispers, gossip, and innuendo blew freely around Mandan, as freely as the leaves down Main Street in any October. Marilyn knew there was a group of women who even blamed her for what had happened to Christoph—to Christoph! She felt her scarlet letter, felt its blood-red ink upon her every time she was forced to go into town. They stared. They murmured. They laughed. They judged. But these women were the least of her crosses to bear in the aftermath, the men, at least some of them, were insufferable. The catcalls. The whistles. The winks. The vulgarity. To them she was a harlot clearly ready and willing to please them, to satisfy their carnal desires. In the past four years, she had gone out on just one date. Harold Spence—an immature, innocuous, harmless man if there ever were one, who worked at the depot sweeping up—picked her up, drove around the block, parked and began pawing at her. He was still missing the tooth she had knocked out when she punched him with all her might.

Karl looked like an angel. He looked older than she remembered. She could see the stubble on his face, something she had never seen before for he had always been clean- shaven and well-groomed. She liked it. It looked manly. His hair was matted and cropped short now, unlike the stylish coif he had once sported. Again, it suited him and she liked his new shorter style.

Marilyn could sense the smile on her face. She felt like a woman again, not a thing. She knew she looked good because she had been primping all week for this moment; had even chanced going to town to the beauty parlor where the beautician had given her the latest, most modern, and sophisticated of hairdos possible. Her lipstick was a bright, fun, almost too sexy red and she fantasized about kissing Karl until his face was entirely covered with little kisses in the shape of her lips. She was ready and raised two fingers from the glass her palm rested against

She was just about to tap on the window to wake him when an Indian woman about her own age entered the room, fussed with this and fussed with that, straightening up, before she leaned over Karl, kissed him on the forehead and switched off the reading lamp at the side of his chair. The room went dark and so did Marilyn's heart.

Later she could not recall running to her car or driving home through the night, but in the morning, back at home, sitting alone in a bathrobe, her lipstick smeared, and the remnants of her mascara still running with her tears down her cheeks, the memory of that strange woman's lips upon the forehead of her Perseus was running circles around her brain beneath her fashionable hairdo still sitting uselessly atop her head.

CHAPTER SEVENTY

Somewhere between Williston and Fargo, North Dakota (2011)

The drive across US-52 going east was going to take Charlie about seven hours with stops. Despite the boom, there was still a whole lot of nothing along the 392 miles between Williston and Fargo except for the city of Minot at the 126 mile mark. It was going to be a long day. It was true he could have just called this Norman Ehrlich, the Cummins legal department had done a bang up job helping his father's attorney track down the mystery man. Charlie had not only the address, but the phone number as well. But he needed to know for himself who he had shared in the spoils with and more importantly, maybe find out why. He had never heard the name before and Owen Harris, Esq. said that the name had been one of the final and late changes to the will made by Karl. At any rate, there would be plenty of time to think about who Norman Ehrlich could be and what his connection to Charlie's father was on the mind-numbing drive across the state. Charlie was on the road in pursuit of the last piece of the puzzle his father had left behind before he could leave behind Williston for good this time.

CHAPTER SEVENTY-ONE

Mandan, North Dakota (1946-47)

*

"Man is not what he thinks he is, he is what he hides."

- André Malraux

*

John Paul Hoff had been poised between 1946 and 1947 to write his own ticket in regards to his political future in North Dakota and maybe beyond the confines of his oft maligned state, perhaps in Washington, D.C. itself. His connections to congressman, generals, and the Democratic Party, which he had joined after becoming a citizen, were impressive. But his passion for the Constitution and the rights of all men, including the Indian tribes of his great state, put him at odds with progressive agendas of the White House and of Democrats pushing for progress in North Dakota and all along the banks of the Missouri Valley via the Garrison Dam project. He couldn't get behind it and wouldn't. He held his citizenship up in front of those who confronted him about his vocal denunciations of the dam. How was it that he, an immigrant, could become a citizen and yet the original inhabitants of this country had to suffer a second class citizenship? How could his rights be more than theirs?

It didn't make sense, so he threw himself into the role of being a voice for those who could not be heard; in this case, the Three Affiliated Tribes whose land was going to be taken from them by government decree for a supposed monetary compensation John Paul viewed as nothing less than outright theft; a check for their troubles, a money-green paint job to cover over white guilt about more broken promises and broken treaties. But the unraveling of his dreams of walking the hallowed halls of the District of Columbia one day was actually rooted not in his beliefs, but in his actions.

*

John Paul had a secret, a secret he took to his deathbed with him. But while he was alive, it haunted his conscience without sympathy, no matter how he tried to rationalize it. He hated Frank Lund, but what he hated more was how Frank disregarded and humiliated Eleanor without regret. John Paul had lost his wife, a woman he loved with all his heart, but whom had become another person over the course of their marriage and whose grip on reality slipped through her hands until it was no longer there for her to hold onto. Having her committed to the state hospital in Jamestown had been the hardest thing he had ever done in his life. The fact that it was all due to some or another mental illness, didn't make it any less painful. And here was Frank, running around on a good woman, a woman in complete control of her mental faculties, but a woman who John Paul came to know was suffering, confused, and depressed just like so many of the patients wandering the halls and tied to beds in North Dakota State Hospital. Yes, unlike them, she was free, but freedom is a state of mind more than anything. She was not free and would not be until she was free of Frank.

John Paul had first begun talking with Eleanor at the Elks after he had committed his wife. She lent a sympathetic ear at dinners hosted by the lodge which he now attended stag. Frank could have cared less who his wife talked to or when or where, but especially when he was holding court at the Elks bar. He flirted with the waitresses, pinched their bottoms, swore a blue streak, and generally made a spectacle of himself while poor Eleanor tried to smile through a cringe or a grimace.

At first they just talked at these types of social gatherings, infrequently but intensely. He knew of her reputation as a spendthrift, but the more he talked to her and the more often he talked to her, he could see that she was only trying to distract herself from her own intense loneliness and sense of abandonment by Frank. She even blamed herself for his carousing, which John Paul told her was ludicrous.

Frank's house was close to Main Street in Mandan and often Eleanor walked into town rather than taking the ridiculously large car Frank had bought for her. He was always buying Eleanor a new ridiculously big car, though she wasn't all that good at driving. It was on such an occasion when she had walked into town to do a little shopping that John Paul spotted her on the sidewalk. He was on his way to Bismarck for a meeting, but could not help himself and on a whim that surprised both of them, he pulled to the curb and asked her if she needed a ride.

"No. But I'll take one."

That was the first time he made love to her in Frank's house, but not the last.

It was scandalous and they both knew it, but neither cared. She was passionate and funny and John Paul found himself letting his own guard down. He was funny too. He'd never known it, but he was. She loved his stories and he loved to hear her laugh. It was a schoolgirl's laugh. The reality was when they were together they were both able to put aside the little hells that followed them. Her little hells were those Frank made for her and John Paul's were full of demons whispering in his ear that he could have done more for his wife, had been too quick to commit her. John Paul and Eleanor's mutual fire, a lustful fire, a giddy fire, reduced to ash their personal torments.

But they were dancing with the devil.

CHAPTER SEVENTY-TWO
Williston, North Dakota (1952)

Karl had become increasingly distant from Elsie. When he was home, he spent from dawn to nightfall in the fields, but in the past year he'd also been making frequent trips to Lund Cement's headquarters in Garrison to rebuild relationships, drum up new business and to bring a critical eye to the books, paying off the large debts the company had been carrying while moving the moderate but improving cash flow into investments both outside the business and within. He didn't want to do it, but when one of the top managers called twelve months earlier to say that Frank had gone missing and the business was teetering on the edge of a complete financial collapse, he decided then to take a more active role in the business he owned but had never operated, telling friends and associates in Williston it was to honor his father's memory and the hard work he had done to establish the company in the first place.

Elsie was alone most of the time now and she put away her dream of having children or at least on hold until Karl got things under control in Garrison. She knew why Frank had 'gone missing' but that too she had put away. That was blood between brothers and there was a whole Lund family history she really knew nothing about. It was not hard for her to rationalize away; Karl had told her a few years earlier that he thought Frank had killed their little brother, Christoph, and gotten away with it.

Though she tried to occupy herself with some watercolor painting here, some piano lesson there, she missed her old routine of domestic chores since Karl had hired what amounted to a staff to tend to the day-to-day details of keeping a home. Thankfully none of them lived at the house, but travelled in each day from Williston and the surrounding, smaller farm communities to do their work in and around the Lund farmhouse which was forever being renovated and expanded by a few trusted workmen. Then, of course, there was the seasonal help during harvest time. All in all, it had become a madhouse. It had forever been just she and her father. If by some miracle he were to return one day, he wouldn't recognize his own home, she thought.

Her mother came to mind more and more, kindling a renewed interest in her heritage. Unbeknownst to Karl, she had begun to take trips to Parshall where her mother had grown up on the reservation which was now having its boundaries redrawn by the big dam project. A few of her mother's relatives still lived on 'The Rez' as almost everyone called it and they were welcoming and warm to her. When she did visit she spent the day helping as much with cleaning and cooking as she could, more out of selfish desire to do those things than a sense of obligation. And she played with the children who were always running around outside, making mischief or simply enjoying the carefree and secure atmosphere that was somehow still cultivated in the poor, but close-knit communities of the Fort Berthold Reservation.

There was also a handsome, young Arikara man who lived just down from her cousins and who paid her much attention when she was out hanging laundry or beating rugs. The day he came by on an old, rickety bicycle with big, but flat tires and gave her a daisy, which were everywhere in the weedy yards, she did not say a thing but turned away from him instead and ran into the little house, her face flush and hot.

Still, she missed Karl and longed for a return to the life they had led in the months just after they were married, a simple but satisfying life full of only one another.

CHAPTER SEVENTY-THREE
Fargo, North Dakota (2011)

The house was modest with a tiny, well-trimmed lawn surrounded by a small, decorative fence. There was a man standing in the yard picking up small, bare branches felled by a recent thunderstorm. He looked to be in his late fifties or early sixties and had a full head of silver hair, well-trimmed just like the yard. He stood just over six feet tall perhaps and had a strong build for his age. *So, this is Norman Ehrlich*, Charlie thought.

Norman Ehrlich, a bundle of sticks still in his hand, stared at the pickup which had pulled into his driveway. Charlie got out and was immediately greeted with a curt, "How can I help you?" which seemed a polite way of saying, *Who the fuck are you and what are you doing in my driveway?*

"Name's Charlie Lund."

"So?"

"My father was Karl Lund of Williston."

"And?"

"Well, it seems you're in his will. You're Norman Ehrlich, right?"

Norman turned toward the house and called out, "Maggie, call the police."

Charlie put his hands up as though he were being arrested and walked forward a few steps, shouting, "Don't do that. I'm not kidding about the will." Then reaching into his back pocket he produced a copy of it which he held in the air, wiggling it in Norman's direction. "Here. Look for yourself."

Norman dropped the sticks and walked forward slowly, bending to pick up a rusty hedge clipper from the lawn as he approached.

"You're not going hit me or stab me with that thing, are you?

Norman didn't answer, but did swipe the document from Charlie's hand. He stepped back and pulled a pair of reading glasses from the breast pocket of his heavy work shirt.

"It's the fourth page in and it's highlighted."

The man flipped a few pages and began to read.

"That's your address and phone number on that document, isn't it?"

Again, Norman didn't answer.

He finished reading and flipped through some of the other pages before stepping forward and holding it out for Charlie to take back which Charlie did.

"What the hell do you want?"

"Nothing really," Charlie replied. "You see the thing is that document says you now own half my father's land along with me. It's worth a lot of money, sits on top of a lot of oil, but I'd like to give it to my son."

"So give it to him."

"I need your signature."

"Not likely, Tonto." Then Norman shouted, "Maggie," again.

"Listen, Mr. Ehrlich, let me spell it out for you. You're entitled to half the profits of a sale or half the value of the property according to this will. It's notarized and everything. Or if there were ever a lease deal with an oil company, well, you'd be a rich man."

Norman stepped forward, looking incensed.

"Oil? Williston? Yeah, I've read all about that shit out there. You couldn't pay me."

"Can I ask why?"

"You can if you get the fuck off my property."

"Fair enough. Why?"

"That deal is a shit mess out there. From what I hear, Williston's full of dope, drug dealers, and prostitutes now. I read the papers. No. Thank. You. I don't want nothin' to do with that shit hole. Get my name off that document, whatever it is."

"I'll let them know," Charlie reassured before adding, "And thank you."

"For what?"

"Perspective."

And with that enlightening exchange behind him, Charlie turned to get in his pickup, but paused, turning back.

"How did you know my father?"

Annoyed, Norman shot back, "I said one question."

Charlie stood his ground. "You wanna call Maggie again or just answer the question?

"I didn't. Don't know who the hell he is or who you are. Now leave or I'll get my shotgun."

"I believe you would," Charlie confirmed without a speck of sarcasm and then got into his pickup and left. He couldn't believe he was looking forward to getting back to Williston. The people in Fargo *were* as strange as in that movie.

CHAPTER SEVENTY-FOUR
Mandan, North Dakota (1947/48)

John Paul's affair with Eleanor had been going on for almost nine months by the fall of 1947 and he knew she was getting antsy. All summer she had been pestering him to tell Frank of the affair and that she wanted a divorce. She couldn't bring herself to do it. She feared his reaction. John Paul feared it as well, but it wasn't just that. He had a responsibility to his wife, though he knew she would never come home again. Of greater concern was his responsibility to his daughter. Mandan was a small town where people did know one another and people talked. He was not prepared to drag Marilyn through the mud of a scandal. Were he to set that in motion, he was sure it would be a topic of gossip in a town known for its gossip and that it would follow her for a long time. *The daughter of the adulterer.* He could hear it already.

The more Eleanor pressured him, the further he withdrew from her and the idea of a life together. He loved the regular tumbles in the hay, but he couldn't bear the thought of the burden Marilyn would have to shoulder if he continued letting his privates lead him down this path. He knew he had to break it off. Not only would there be personal consequences if he didn't stop, there were already professional setbacks which had come from the amount of time he had dedicated to her in the past six months. His name was coming up less and less at the political roundtables across the state. The Garrison Dam position had cost him, no doubt, but it was his love-struck countenance which had cost him his momentum. Eleanor, for all her good heartedness, was a major distraction. But what made him most uncomfortable with and reflective upon the whole situation was the fact that he had begun lying to Marilyn, saying he was going here or there when he was really with Eleanor.

The monthly poker games at the Elks were just one of the smoke screens he had been deploying. But it was for good reasons that he lied to Marilyn just one last time when October's installment of the poker game arrived. As was usual now, he wouldn't be there; he'd be with Eleanor for Frank never missed a poker game. Ironically, Frank would miss this one, because he had headed to Stanton with Karl to wet his whistle and make some whoopee. John Paul would lie to Marilyn only so he could meet Eleanor and break it off with her.

He kissed Marilyn on the forehead before he left and asked her what her plans were for the evening. She was more dressed up than usual but told him she had nothing planned. But soon after John Paul left, she began looking out for Karl's car; they had a secret date planned.

At Eleanor's, John Paul went through the motions, hugging, kissing, making all lovey- dovey with her while he waited for his courage to arrive so that he could tell her he couldn't do this anymore. But things headed in that direction when she pulled back from one of his kisses and announced, "I'm going to tell Frank about us."

*

"Don't be ridiculous, Eleanor. This is not the right time."

"For you or for me?"

John Paul knew she had spunk and that was as good a question as any. He'd always thought of himself as an honest man. But he also knew that all the liars in the world would say the same. He had never promised her directly that they would get married, perhaps indirectly. *What were promises anyway?* Words about intended actions, he supposed, but he lived in the world, she did not. He understood that promises were made and broken everyday. Broken promises were at the heart of his objection to the dam. He had promised, Eleanor, but he also knew that honesty was the best policy. Then again, he was a politician. Diplomacy was an option, but compromise was probably not.

In the end, he simply went with a good, old fashioned scare tactic.

"I'm afraid Frank will kill you if you tell him about us."

She saw right through it.

"Frank? Ha. Are you afraid of Frank, John Paul? Is that it?"

John Paul shook his head from side to side. Then he thought of Marilyn, whom he should have been thinking of all along. He was doing this for her, even if it was hard for him. He stood.

"Eleanor, I am not afraid of Frank. What I am afraid of is that I have made a terrible mistake in letting my emotions get the better of me. You are a married woman. This town is very small. My daughter…"

But he didn't finish because Eleanor had cut him off and was now standing toe-to-toe with him.

"Your daughter? Your daughter? What about me, John Paul?"

Then she stepped back and her entire face squinted, pulling her full lips into thin red lines. His reticence was not due to anything she had considered before, had wanted to consider, but now it was clear. Now she was demanding action, not promises. She felt used, for he would not be honoring his promises, nor would he be taking action.

She turned and walked toward the front door, pausing to wrap a shawl around her shoulders and to grab a clutch from a small table in the foyer.

"What are you doing?" John Paul asked, nervous and walking slowly but emphatically toward her.

"I'm going to the Elks."

"Why, Eleanor?"

"Why do you think, Mr. Hoff?"

She reached for the doorknob and he lunged for her.

Passion is just anger on good behavior. And as they rolled and tumbled in the foyer, knocking over a coat rack, a floor lamp, and an umbrella stand, Eleanor bit and scratched and punched John Paul as he tried not to hurt her, but to contain her. This went on for another minute until, exhausted by her and disgusted with himself, he let go of her wrists and fell back, ending up slumped against the wall.

The foyer was filled with the sound of their panting. Eleanor tried to lift her slightly plump frame from the floor.

"Let me help you," John Paul offered as he attempted to rise.

On her knees now she spun to him and spit, "Don't... you... touch... me."

Through his panting, John Paul, moved to compromise, offering, "Eleanor, please don't tell Frank. Let me talk to him. I'll tell him."

"I'm not going to tell Frank," she baited him.

"You're not?"

Eleanor was on her feet and looking down at John Paul who was only to his knees.

"No. I'm going to tell your daughter."

She stepped around him and walked out the door. He followed after her, but when he noticed a neighbor next door smoking a cigarette on his porch, Hoff backed off and mumbled, "Have a good evening," to a scowling Eleanor, before heading up the sidewalk to his car some blocks away.

Eleanor composed herself, bid the neighbor a curt, "Good night," and walked back inside to await Frank's arrival home from his poker game. But he never did come home that night. Or at all the next day. Two days later, the word was all over town that Christoph had raped the Hoff girl and Christoph had shot himself out at the cabin.

She would not be telling Marilyn about her father's affair. And when months later she told Frank, he said he didn't care...thought they made a lovely couple. It was then she filed for divorce. A few months after the divorce, lonely and alone, she got up the nerve to see John paul again. She missed him and she was now free to do as she pleased. But she had behaved badly, so it was with much trepidation on a cold March morning that she entered the hardware store where John Paul now worked.

But when she approached him, quietly saying how sorry she was for what Christoph had done to Marilyn, he simply looked up from his brooming of the floor and asked, "May I help you, ma'am?" as if he didn't even know her.

A few months later she headed back to Wisconsin to her parents' house where she lived out the rest of her life as a spinster, squandering the alimony Frank sent each month on mail-order junk from the Sears catalog which often went unopened—until a few years later the checks just stopped coming.

CHAPTER SEVENTY-FIVE

Williston, North Dakota (2011)

Two police cars were parked off the shoulder of Highway 1804 in front of the house, a North Dakota 'statie' and a cruiser from Williston shone in the pickup's headlights. Charlie had spent fourteen hours in the car to find out that the mystery man in Fargo was just some asshole. It was past midnight. *Now what?*

He took the pickup down a gear, slowing until he made the left between the two police vehicles and into the driveway. He had no more shut off the engine and the lit end of a long flashlight was poking through the open window and blinding him.

"You Charlie Lund?"

Charlie reached for his wallet, but stopped as quickly as he could when the cop, who he couldn't see because of the stun light flooding the pickup, started shouting, "Get your hands where I see'um!"

By the time Charlie brought his hands back to the wheel, lying them palms up across the top, there was a gun to go along with the light poking through the window.

*

At the Williston police station, Charlie sat in a small room talking with the young detective he had given such a hard time to the day of his father's murder and another detective who was older and overweight in comparison.

The fat one did the talking at first.

"Did your wife have a motive to kill your father?"

"My wife?"

The young detective spoke up.

"Shannon Dilfer. Did Shannon Dilfer have a motive?"

"You tell me," Charlie volleyed back.

The young detective composed himself and continued.

"It's true there was an incident the day before where she threatened to kill him, but I am going to ask you again. Did she have a motive?"

Charlie found the whole discussion laughable. After a week of dragging their feet, this was the interrogation?

The fat detective jumped in.

"Answer the question. You waived the right to counsel. Now answer the question."

"Who didn't have a motive?" Charlie posed back to them.

"So that's a yes?" the young detective asked.

"I guess it would be if that's the way you're hearing it."

The two detectives put their heads together and whispered back and forth just briefly, after which the young detective stood and announced, "Okay, then. Detective Pullen will write up your statement. When you sign it, you're free to go."

"My statement?"

The young detective did not answer, but just stood and waited as Detective Pullen sat writing up the statement. Finished, he slid it toward Charlie and handed him the pen.

"John Hancock right there at the bottom with the date."

Charlie picked up the pen. This was a parody of a bad cop drama. He was tired and had planned to leave in the morning, maybe make his way to Hawaii via California. He signed the paper, handed the pen back, stood, and walked out the door.

Prairie justice is alive and well, he thought as he left the police station.

The night was warm as he walked out of town and made his way to Highway 1804. He stuck his thumb out occasionally as a car or truck passed. It reminded him of how he had bummed around the country when things got lean and he had to sell whatever junker he owned at the time. He wasn't feeling nostalgic, just a sense of wonder and bemusement at the thought of how moving forward is the only way to get somewhere. *Just keep moving*, he thought.

A little further down the highway a semi stopped to pick him up. Unbelievably, the 18-wheeler had Florida plates. Charlie laughed to himself and then stepping out into the road waved the trucker to go on without him. The trucker stuck his head out the window twisting his neck, looking back at Charlie.

He yelled into the night air above the idling of the big diesel rig, "You got an ugly face, injun" and then dropped it into gear and shuddered away in fits and starts of clutch and gas, clutch and gas.

Maybe, Charlie thought, *but at least I know it's mine now.*

EPILOGUE 1

Blood

CHAPTER SEVENTY-SIX
Williston, North Dakota (2011)

After leaving Karl Lund's place, the debacle of the land sale and melee that followed still fresh in their minds, the two Cummins Energy men who'd been humiliated by the old man, made their way to Room 119, Dawes' room at the motel. The bleary-eyed, junkie derrick hand they both knew all too well opened the door, startled from his sleep by their tandem pounding.

"Let's have a talk, Dawes," one of them said and Dawes dropped his arm from the doorjamb and let them enter.

*

It was just after midnight when Dawes jimmied the old lock of the backdoor of Karl Lund's large farmhouse. The home which had been added onto almost endlessly over the decades was a maze of interconnecting hallways. Dawes got lost at one point and ended up back at the door he'd jimmied. Another hallway he wandered ended in a dead end, but finally Dawes found the living room the two Cummins men had described. And, there sat Karl Lund in a chair facing away from him. He couldn't tell if the old man was awake or asleep, but then Karl Lund spoke, asking in a phlegm-choked voice, "Who's there?"

Dawes pulled a buck knife from his belt line, moved lightly, one step at a time, over the course of almost a minute, crossing the ten feet that had stood between them until he was at the back of the chair.

Twenty minutes later Dawes was having a beer at the 4 Mile Bar.

EPILOGUE 2
Oil

CHAPTER SEVENTY-SEVEN

Williston, North Dakota (2012)

Excavators and dump trucks from Cummins Energy dotted the former Lund property's substantial acreage. Field managers directed different stages of drilling, rigging, and site prep. Two excavators were working an area that had been pasture at one time and had just begun to dig into the soft spring ground, the beginnings of a huge retention pond for a nearby frack site. One of them stopped after hitting something that didn't give, but then dug right back in deeper with the toothed bucket for a scoop full of sod and dirt. When the operator pulled back the boom, lifting the arm, a car began to rise into the air, the bucket sticking through where the front windshield had been. In the trunk of Frank's earth-caked Delahaye 135 convertible, his skeleton was waiting to be found.

Frank's hunch about Williston and buying land where some believed there might be oil had been a prescient one. And now, here he was, over seven decades later, a silent witness to the plundering of one of the biggest petroleum plays in North America.

EPILOGUE 3

Water

CHAPTER SEVENTY-EIGHT

Garrison Dam Closure Ceremonies (June 11, 1953)

*

"Everywhere there will be need for the power, for the controls of flood waters, for the irrigation water and for the navigation that will travel our streams."
- President Dwight D. Eisenhower
(Garrison Dam Closure Ceremonies Speech)

*

Elsie noticed her husband daydreaming when he should have been listening to President Eisenhower. She was just happy to be there, that Karl had wanted her to be on his arm to witness it all. It was his day. Elsie understood that and so she gave him his moment. She had become used to these types of moments when he could be right beside her, but somehow far away. Not even the President of the United States could break that spell, so how could she think that she ever would be able to either? Looking back to the podium, Elsie felt a rush of pride to be Karl's wife. Looking back forty years on at the end of her life, she would remember this as the single best day of their marriage.

Karl could see the President of the United States, could hear him as he spoke to the assembled crowd at the Garrison Dam Closure Ceremonies, but his mind turned to his brothers, Frank and Christoph, and then to the words which Shakespeare had put in Macbeth's mouth in Act 2, Scene 2: *I am afraid to think what I have done; Look on't again I dare not.* But look he did and all he saw, like Macbeth, was the blood on his hands. Then Lady Macbeth's words came to mind: *A little water clears us this deed.* But Karl knew not even all the Missouri River water corralled behind the Garrison Dam could do that for him.

*   *   *

Made in the USA
Las Vegas, NV
23 October 2021